Avenge Me Daddy

Mafia Daddies NYC

Book 3

Zack Wish

KEEP IN TOUCH

Thank you so much for reading, I hope you enjoy my book!

If you'd love a **steamy & cute FREE STORY**, and lots of *fun updates*, *freebies* and *more*, sign up to my newsletter by clicking the link below:

bit.ly/3KME5ra

I love to hear from readers, so please feel free to email me at zackwishauthor@gmail.com

Stalk me at the places below! Click the links and make sure you don't miss a thing!

Chapter 1

Rex

'Keep... pushing...,' Rex said, using every ounce of energy he had in his body. 'Just one... more... lift.'

Rex just about managed to complete the rep and then gladly let his dumbbells fall to the floor. The rubber coated weights made a thudding noise as the dropped onto the protective matting beneath the bench and Rex was left with a feeling of pure satisfaction.

They weren't exactly heavy weights. Certainly they weren't heavy weights compared to the kinds of sizes that some of the other people in the gym were throwing around. But that didn't matter. Rex was happy with his personal achievement, and that's what counted as far as he was concerned.

Rex was twenty years old and coming to the Rise Up Gym was one of his favorite things to do in his spare time. With his sandy-blonde hair and emerald-green eyes, Rex was already a pretty noticeable figure amongst the larger, far more gruff men who usually occupied the free weights section.

The fact that Rex also had a dangling little strawberry earring in one ear and also had a penchant for brightly colored workout clothes just made him stand out all the more.

Rex didn't mind standing out from the crowd though. Rise Up Gym had a very clear policy that everyone was to be treated with fairness and respect. There would be no passive-aggressive or rude behavior tolerated at Rise Up, and Rex felt comfortable to be himself there.

After wiping down his bench, Rex stood up and checked his phone. After swiping away a few app notifications, Rex saw that he had received a message from his manager at the *Peachy Playpen...*

Hey, Rex. Thanks again for agreeing to do that extra shift today. Just wanted to double check that you're still good to come in? And YES, we still do have some birthday cake leftover from yesterday for staff to snack on! Stevey.

Rex grinned. The thought of having some deliciously colorful and frosting-covered cake to munch on during his work shift was something to look forward to, that was for sure.

Cake! Yummy!

As if work wasn't fun enough already.

But maybe I should do some extra cardio in preparation?

Rex actually loved working at the *Peachy Playpen*. It was one of the best spots in the whole city for Littles to come to and have fun, go wild, or simply chill. In other words, if you were a

Little and wanted to express yourself totally unselfconsciously, then the *Peachy Playpen* was the place to be.

The Peachy Playpen had a craft room, changing and diaper facilities, nap time snuggle areas and a whole lot more too. It was just perfect. And it was especially perfect for Rex because he was a Little too.

New York City may have been an enormous, diverse city but not everyone understood what a Little was. Some people could even make judgmental or mean comments about it when they found out. So having a place like the *Peachy Playpen* was essential.

Each and every Little was different. Some Littles liked to focus on age regression and relax and play until they regressed all the way back and needed to wear diapers. For other Littles, the age regression was less and it was more about being able to have innocent fun playing with toys and stuffies, or perhaps spending time doing craft.

Everyone was covered at the *Peachy Playpen*. Rex loved to see the Littles and their Daddies having a wonderful time together. Rex didn't have a Daddy, but he was beginning to wish he did. The idea of having a big, strong man to look after him was appealing in the extreme. The only problem was that Rex just hadn't met the right man who would sweep him off his feet.

Perhaps Rex's lack of a Daddy was also down to his refusal to take anything in life too seriously. Whether it was career aspirations, bedtimes, or relationships, everything was to be taken in a lighthearted, casual way as far as Rex was concerned. This super-relaxed attitude also applied to his shift start times, much to the annoyance of his bosses at the *Peachy Playpen*.

Rex knew he didn't have long left at the gym, but he still felt like he was having too much fun to leave. Rex cast his eye around the gym's vast floorspace and his eyes settled on the long row of treadmills. Seconds later, Rex was up and running on the treadmill. He may have been on a tight time limit, but if there was going to be cake and treats at work, he had to get the calories worked off in advance.

Having completed the first cardio blast, Rex should have hopped off and headed straight to the changing room. But feeling good from one sprint workout, Rex simply couldn't resist another...

I guess I'd better hit the showers now.

I am on a warning at work for tardiness after all.

LOL, just one more bit of cardio won't do any harm!

* * *

'*Phew*!' Rex said, casually walking into the locker room with a big smile on his face having just beaten his previous personal best on the treadmill's sprint triple-challenge. 'I am... beat!'

Rex was dripping with sweat and ready to hit the shower, that was for sure. But as Rex began to strip down, he couldn't help but notice that the locker room was suddenly full of other guys coming in for their showers too.

Unlike Rex, these guys were all on the larger side. Taller, broader, and with the kind of shoulders and biceps that could have been mistaken for boulders and granite rocks, these were seriously impressive men.

But it wasn't just the men's bodies that Rex was interested in.

Rex had a thing for sportswear. In fact, Rex would have said that sportwear was his number one kink, outside of age play. The sight of burly men in their tight shorts and sweaty lycra t-shirts was something that just did it for Rex.

And the longer the men in their hot, sweaty sportswear were around Rex, the harder it was for Rex to not get visibly aroused.

Gulp.

I think I need to get into that shower.

If I don't, I think my dick might just start drawing too much attention...

Before his cock could get any harder, Rex rapidly covered himself up in is large, fluffy yellow towel and hurried inside one of the private shower cubicles.

After rapidly shutting the door behind him and turning the shower on, Rex was soon happily washing away the sweat and giving his tired body some much needed refreshment under the shower's hot water.

But Rex's mind was still very much focused on the men outside. Rex began to wonder if any of them were Daddies. They certainly had the look for it, and Rex couldn't help but imagine what it would feel like if one of them burst into his shower cubicle right there and then and gave his wet bottom a good, hard spanking...

Rex giggled at the thought of his wet butt cheeks being spanked by a gruff man in nothing but a pair of tiny shorts, or even just a pure-white jockstrap.

Rex wasn't entirely sure where his love of guys in sportswear came from. It probably dated back a long way, but all that Rex knew was that he found it super-hot. Rex's dream scenario was a strong, gruff man in a wrestling leotard. The super-tight fit that left nothing to the imagination and the tight, soft, stretchy material was something that never failed to excite Rex.

Two Daddies, both in wrestling suits...

Taking it in turns to spank my butt...

OMG... so freakin' hot!

However as fun as it was to fantasize, Rex grudgingly knew that he was already super-late for work. If he spent any more time daydreaming, he may as well not even bother showing up at the Peachy Playpen at all.

After washing off the remaining soap on his slender, toned body, Rex left the shower and began to get changed into his clothes.

As Rex was rummaging around in his sports bag, he was met with a comforting sight. Snuggled deep inside his long, bright-red sports bag was Ozzy. Rex looked at Ozzy and smiled. Ozzy was Rex's cherished, super-favorite stuffie.

With his big, bushy eyebrows and black and white markings, Ozzy was just about the cuddliest, snuggliest cat in the whole world. Well, that was certainly true as far as Rex was concerned.

Rex and Ozzy had been partners in crime for many, many years. And with Ozzy's love of long naps and taking it easy, they certainly made a great pair together.

For a split second, Rex debated whether or not to take Ozzy out of the gym bag to give him a cuddle. It was possible that someone might see him and start laughing or call him a name.

While Rise Up Gym was well known for its progressive policies, it certainly wasn't perfect. There was nothing to say that someone might see Rex cuddling his stuffie and decide that a good insult or snarky comment was in order.

But Rex liked to take risks.

In that moment, Rex wanted to give his prized stuffie a big, wholesome cuddle. If someone stinky saw him and decided to laugh, well that was a risk that Rex was prepared to take...

'I love you, Ozzy!' Rex said, taking Ozzy out of the bag and bringing his cuddly cat in for one big squeeze. 'I love you to the stars and back!'

Luckily, no one saw Rex giving Ozzy a cuddle. Or if they did, they simply didn't say anything. The risk had paid off. For Rex though, taking risks was just something he did.

Ever since Rex's father sadly passed away, Rex was determined to not let anything hold him back from having fun. And if that meant taking a risky choice, then Rex was pretty much always up for doing that.

Sure, Rex's decisions had sometimes landed him in hot water, but so far it was nothing so bad that it served to change his approach to life. As far as Rex was concerned, if there was a chance to have fun he was going to take it.

Speaking of fun, Rex looked at his watch. He was definitely going to be late for the start of his shift at the Peachy Playpen, but if he hustled, he might be able to sneak in before anyone noticed...

* * *

The *Peachy Playpen* was as busy as ever.

New York was a big city, and the kind of place where there was always enough people to fill up somewhere that catered to a group of people's needs. With its brightly painted walls with the most beautifully stenciled illustrations, the reception area was full of life.

Fortunately for Rex, he had managed to scoot across from the gym and to work just in time. It wasn't even a case of sneaking in, Rex actually made it on time. Well, on time as far as Rex considered it.

Rex's boss Stevey saw it *slightly* differently...

'Only ten minutes late,' Stevey said, flicking his rainbow-colored bangs to one side. 'Well, it's better than an hour late!'

Stevey burst out into laughter and gave Rex a pat on the back. Stevey had been working at the *Peachy Playpen* since day one and was generally an easy-going boss who was always there for his staff when they needed to talk or express a concern.

That wasn't to say that Stevey didn't know how to put his foot down at times too, though. And if Rex thought that he was going to completely get away with being ten minutes late for his shift then he had another thing coming.

'Okay, so, I know how much you just love doing the daily drinks inventory,' Stevey said, standing with his hands on his hips and his fingers hooked into the belt loops of his jean shorts.

'Oh no! Please no!' Rex said, rolling his eyes in mock disgust. 'Not the inventory!'

'Ha! Well, try getting here on time and you might not get left with doing it,' Stevey said. 'You can work reception for a bit, but I need the inventory done in the next couple of hours, okay?'

'Yup, you got it,' Rex said, sarcastically but playfully doing a double thumbs up to his boss. 'I'll get right on it!'

Rex and Stevey exchanged a warm-hearted smile. They may have been employee and boss, but ultimately they were good friends. This was just another thing about working at the Peachy Playpen that Rex enjoyed.

All the staff got along so well together. That wasn't to say that there were no disagreements. But if there ever was a problem, and this was rare, then people would simply talk about it and make things right. There was no sniping or back-biting at the Peachy Playpen, which made it a truly wonderful place to work at.

As the shift progressed, Rex did indeed do the inventory as requested by Stevey. It was as boring as ever, and Rex wasn't overly keen on sitting in the storeroom looking through stock levels and counting up each individual juice box.

However, someone had to do the inventory. And on that particular day it was Rex. Once he was finished, Rex clicked submit on the iPad and walked back out into the reception area.

As Rex took his place at the reception desk, his eyes were immediately drawn to a group of guys who were just entering…

'*Wowzers*,' Rex said, mumbling the words under his breath.

The group of men were all tall, broad shouldered, and wearing dark t-shirts with tight pants. The men had tattooed arms and necks and seemed to be giving off the vibe that they owned the place…

They look a bit scary.

But fun too.

I wonder who they are…

Rex didn't have to ponder the identity of the men for long. One of the men, clearly the group's leader, caught Rex's eye and made a beeline for him at the reception desk.

'The name's Vialli,' the man said, lifting his black Armani shades off his eyes. 'Kash Vialli. You've maybe heard of me?'

'Um… m-m-m-*maybe*?' Rex said, tripping over his words a little.

Kash Vialli, whoever he was, was certainly a striking figure. He must have been early thirties and had the darkest brown eyes and jet-black hair. With his dark, highly tailored suit he was dressed differently to the other men in the group but he certainly had the same level of swagger – if not more.

Rex's eyes were drawn to Kash's diamond encrusted gold watch. Rex wasn't especially into that kind of thing, but the watch was so bright it was impossible not to look.

'I've got plenty more of these,' Kash said, grinning. 'Just don't ask me how I pay for them...'

Rex felt his heart flutter. He couldn't tell if Kash was a nice guy or not. There was something dangerous about Kash, an edge to him that was provoking a reaction in Rex.

'I... I... um, how can I help you?' Rex said, feeling himself blush. 'Are you a member here, or?'

Kash shot his group of friends a look and burst out laughing.

'A member? No,' Kash replied, licking his lips. 'But I'd maybe like to be. I mean, I definitely would if all the boys here are as sweet as you.'

Rex didn't know what to say. This situation was a bit on the intense side. Rex looked around for Stevey, but then remembered that Stevey was on a conference call with the Peachy Playpen's sister business over in LA.

Is Kash flirting with me?

I'm not sure I know what to think of him.

But he is sexy though...

'Well, if you want me to give you a tour, I'm happy to,' Rex finally said, his voice trembling with excitement.

'I've got a better idea,' Kash said. 'Let *me* give *you* a tour. Let's bust out of this place and party.'

Rex didn't know what to say. His shift was due to end, but he barely knew Kash. Hanging out with strange older men wasn't something that Rex was in the habit of doing.

On the other hand, Kash was new, and he was exciting. The way he dressed, his confidence, it all added up to a compelling case in his favor.

And after all, life was all about taking risks, *right*?

Chapter 2

Marco

The sound of cars honking their horns, delivery trucks chugging away, and large steels clattering over on the new skyscraper was quickly silenced as Marco Santino shut the balcony door of his grand penthouse apartment.

'Fuck *that* noise,' Marco said, his gravelly voice in full effect. 'I need some peace and quiet right now.'

Marco locked his balcony door behind him and walked into the apartment's main living area. It was an old building, one of the classic grand old apartment blocks in the entire city.

Apartments rarely changed hands in No.33 Rockway Avenue, and when they did it was usually for figures of at least twenty million. The ongoing gentrification of New York had seen prices skyrocket even higher, and given that Marco was in possession of one of the three penthouses, there was no telling what his place was worth.

Not that Marco was thinking about selling. Far from it, in fact. Marco was more than happy to have his own private kingdom.

The penthouse was extra secure, super-private, and allowed Marco the time and space to plot out his moves and business projects.

Except, when it came to business, Marco wasn't exactly involved in a traditional industry. Nor was Marco a tech bro. Or some kind of investment banker.

The truth was that Marco was one hundred percent unfiltered and unrepentant member of the Mafia. Not that the word Mafia was spoken much. It was silently acknowledged by those who knew, and for the most part it was the unspoken truth between Marco and his close associates. They were tied in to this way of living for life, and it was very much a case of survival of the fittest.

Marco was forty-five years old and one of the best bank robbers in Mafia history, East or West coast. Despite everything in the world around him becoming more and more based in technology and the online world, Marco was old school.

For Marco, robbing a bank wasn't about stealing online security codes and accessing private trust funds or crypto assets. No, a bank heist was still very much a bank heist in all of its real-life guts and glory.

And why should Marco have considered changing his approach?

In over twenty years of being involved in bank jobs, he hadn't been caught or identified once. It was a record that Marco was proud of, but one that he always assumed would come to an end one day. And when that day came, Marco had always sworn to go out all guns blazing rather than face up to spending the rest of his days rotting behind bars.

Marco wandered over toward the bar area in the corner of the room and poured himself a small whiskey. As he dropped the ice in alongside the finely aged liquor, Marco caught a glimpse of himself in the mirror.

Marco may have been forty-five, but he still retained a youthful look. With his soulfully dark eyes and dark brown hair, Marco was as handsome as they came. The unusual blonde streaks in his hair may have made Marco stand out from the crowd, but so too did his impeccably muscular upper body and torso.

'Not bad for an old dude,' Marco said, a wry smile on his face as his mind turned to far more important matters. 'Now for the Goldstone Corp. job...'

Marco walked barefoot over the polished, perfectly maintained oak floor and into his study. Just like the rest of the apartment, the study was just about the quintessential old money New York as you could imagine. With its high ceilings and dark brown furnishings, it was the definition of old school.

But rather than spending his time admiring the fine etchings and craftmanship in the study, Marco had to get down to some serious planning. Well, that was the plan anyway...

Marco, we need to talk. Isn't it about time you found a boy? We need to do some double dates and that isn't happening with you still single... DANTE.

· · ·

No sooner than Marco had finished reading Dante's message, Marco's other Mafia Daddy friend Rocco decided that he needed to throw his opinion into the mix too...

Yo! Make that triple-dates. Finding Eddie was the best thing that happened to me. Just imagine, we could all take the boys camping upstate? Tell me that ain't fun times. ROCCO.

Marco wasn't in the mood for getting into another conversation about why he still hadn't found his Forever boy yet. While he appreciated that Rocco and Dante had his best intentions at heart, Marco wasn't in the mood for pondering the truth as to why he hadn't been able to let a Little into his life on a serious, long-term basis.

No, what Marco wanted in that moment was to shut the conversation down and get back to the real business of plotting the Goldstone Corp. robbery...

Guys, guys... relax. I'm too fucking busy for this shit. Some of us have... business... to plan. Got it? Talk later. MARCO.

Marco had known he was a Daddy for a long time. It was normal to him, and he was glad to have other close friends who had the same feelings as he did. But despite loving nothing more than giving a boy a paddling, Marco had never even come close to allowing a real relationship to truly flourish.

It wasn't that Marco didn't want to have a boy to call his own, but he just didn't seem capable of making himself vulnerable enough to let someone in all the way.

Maybe it was down to the nature of his work. Looking over his shoulder and trying to predict where danger might lie 24/7 took its toll. With his whole life playing out as a cat and mouse game, Marco had lost the ability to make himself an open book.

This closed approach to his romantic feelings made dating hard. Even if the spark was there with a boy, Marco would find himself keeping a distance. Understandably, this wasn't exactly appealing to the other party, and Marco rarely got beyond the first three or four dates.

Still, Marco was happy with his life for the most part.

Romance, if it was ever going to come, would have to find its own way through his defenses. Marco was determined that his way of living was the only way he was going to ensure that he never lost his edge and got caught out by the cops or a rival gang.

Marco took a sip of his whiskey as he sat down at his desk.

But... if every day could be my last...

Shouldn't I just loosen up and let it all hang out?

Nope. Can't do it. I'm Marco Santino.

* * *

Marco clicked out of his computer's main screen and sent it into a high-security lockdown mode. Given the nature of the details on there, it would have been crazy to not have the absolute highest level of security.

According to the Mafia hacker who had set the computer up, it would take the best FBI and CIA hackers at least five years to break into it. Fifteen or twenty years would have been better, but five years wasn't too bad all things considered.

That being said, Marco always made a habit of not putting every detail of a heist down on his computer. The real, super-vital details were always committed to one place and one place only, and that was Marco's head.

Satisfied that he was making good progress on the plot, Marco leaned back in his chair and then opened up the drawer to his side.

'Damn... looking good,' Marco said. 'And feeling even better...'

Marco was running his hands over several pairs of lacey, super-silky panties. There was something about lingerie and intricate, delicate panties that had always driven Marco wild.

Specifically, Marco liked to wear lingerie. It was his kink, and something that he was comfortable enough about. He wouldn't have shouted it from the rooftops, especially given how macho and brutal the world he operated in was.

But Marco didn't feel ashamed about it either.

If I had a boy, maybe we could share this kink?

Make it fun.

Maybe both wear our panties at home...

As Marco fantasized about life with a boy who loved panties as much as he did, he ran his fingers through a particularly smooth and high cut pair of black panties and felt his long, thick manhood come to life inside his suit pants.

'*Grrrrr*, I don't have time,' Marco said, his cock twitching and hardening at double-speed. 'Maybe later. *Definitely* maybe later...'

With Marco's phone alarm bleeping as loudly and irritatingly as anyone could imagine, Marco realized that it was time to get out of his apartment and hit the gym.

But this wasn't a gym where people lifted weights and cycled on stationary bikes. No, this was an MMA, or mixed martial arts, gym.

It was time for Marco to get panties out of his mind and focus instead on kicking, wrestling and striking his opponents into submission...

* * *

The MMA gym was a world away from the luxury confines of Marco's penthouse. There wasn't a hardwood floor or piece of expensive artwork in sight.

But this was just how Marco liked it.

Living in a luxurious home was all well and good, but Marco had worked his way up from the very bottom and he enjoyed the no-frills, salt of the earth atmosphere at the gym.

As he walked into the main combat gym from the locker room, Marco was hit with the distinctive sight and sound of men grappling, talking smack, and generally pushing themselves to their limits.

'Hell yeah,' Marco said, eyeing up the roster of usual faces who he had come to know and love in the world of mixed martial arts. 'Let's get to fucking work.'

The session passed quickly. It was an intense one-hour workout that was focused on kicks, both from an offensive and defensive perspective. Marco enjoyed it immensely and was glad to work on an aspect of his fighting style that needed some improvement.

When it came to his bank heists, violence was always a last resort – and it normally involved guns too. But Marco was a genuine expert in one on one, unarmed combat, and working on his kicking skills was only going to be of benefit. After all, Marco could never predict when his gun might not be to hand on a bank job.

But not everything was so sweet at the gym.

'Hey, old man, you look like you might have a heart attack?' came the shout from over on the other side of the training area.

Marco knew exactly who it was shouting and calling him out. It was Aleksei Ivanov. To say that Marco and Aleksei weren't the best of friends would have been something of an understatement.

Aleksei was younger, taller, and in many ways he was the more naturally gifted of the two of them when it came to combat sport. The fact that Aleksei was cocky as hell and not afraid of talking trash to Marco was just the icing on this particularly unpleasant cake as far as Marco was concerned.

Marco threw Aleksei a hard stare.

Aleksei Ivanov was a physical specimen, that was for sure. Standing at 6 feet 5 inches, Aleksei towered over most opponents, and he knew how to make his height advantage count too.

While Aleksei may have had a bald, shaved head he was certainly *not* plain looking as the back of his head was covered with a large, Russian gang tattoo. In fact, Aleksei's whole body was a shrine to classic Russian mob art.

Aleksei was cocky, wild and a little bit unstable.

But Marco wasn't afraid of Aleksei. Far from it...

'Go screw yourself, kid,' Marco called back, wiping his face with a hand towel. 'It's you and me in the tournament. We'll see who comes out on top then, fool.'

'Yeah, we will,' Aleksei replied, a sneer on his face. 'You'll tap out for me, don't think I won't make you. Well, unless I choose to knock you out cold. Either way, it's a big W for me and an L for you. Got it?'

Marco shook his head. He felt angry. Aleksei was starting to push things too far. Smack talk in the gym was one thing, and Marco even enjoyed it on occasion. But Aleksei didn't know when to stop. In fact, Aleksei was in danger of going beyond the point of no return.

Aleksei was Russian Mafia. This meant that him and Marco were never likely to be the best of friends. In fact, had they bumped into one another on the streets, the whole situation could have turned sour very quickly indeed.

However, the rule of the MMA gym was that whatever happened in the gym, stayed in the gym. Marco was happy to play along with this, and it was a rule that made sense too. Things could get very heated during training, and it was only right that conflict in the gym didn't spill out into the real world outside.

Marco however had always doubted whether Aleksei felt the same.

There were rumors that Aleksei was getting wilder and wilder in his behavior outside of the gym. Of course, a rumor was far from guaranteed to be the truth, but it was being said that Aleksei was beginning to ignore orders from his higher-ups and taking rivals out without permission.

Still, this was none of Marco's business. If the rumors about Aleksei were true, then that was up to the Russian kings to sort out. All that Marco wanted was to face Aleksei in the gym tournament and come out victorious.

As Aleksei returned to working the heavy bag, Marco watched on. There was no doubting that Aleksei would be tough to beat, but Marco was determined to give it absolutely everything.

That cocky sonofabitch will fall.

I may be older, but I have the IQ.

I'll put that asshole on his ass and have him tapping out if it's the last thing I do...

* * *

The drive over from the MMA gym to Marco's favorite whiskey bar was easier than Marco had anticipated. Maybe it was just one of those days, but all of the lights seemed to be on green and the traffic was uncharacteristically light.

Marco gripped the wheel and weaved around a delivery truck, the handling on his Maserati feeling light and supple. But this wasn't just any old Maserati. This was a one-of-a-kind model that had come straight from the manufacturer, and at an exorbitant extra cost too...

I ain't complaining.

I just need whiskey and some good company.

And the sooner, the better...

As he got nearer to the whiskey bar, Marco found his mind drifting back to Aleksei. It was one thing to say that what went on in the gym should stay there, but that didn't stop Marco from feeling uneasy about the prospect of taking Aleksei on in a fight.

Marco felt good after his workout, but he knew that no matter how hard he trained it was always going to be a difficult task to beat Aleksei.

Defeat wasn't an option. But even if he did lose, Marco knew that he would pull himself up and get on with his life.

Overcoming brutal losses was something that Marco had known in his life ever since the day he witnessed his parents getting murdered as a child. Marco's father was a Mafia man himself, and it was a risk that anyone in the business took.

Marco's father had often told Marco that he might one day go out for work and never return. It had been difficult for Marco to fully get this as a child, but growing up around so many other Mafia kids, it was something that they all had to grasp as best they could.

Marco though had always assumed that his father would be one of the lucky ones who would make it to old age and then be rewarded with a dignified retirement in the suburbs, or maybe even back in the old country.

Still, when it happened, Marco felt like his whole world had been turned upside down. It was horrible.

To witness the death of both of your parents was something that no child needed to see. Marco knew the events of that fateful day in his childhood would likely stay with him forever. There was no way that anyone could see both their mother and father ruthlessly shot and not come away from that with some form of psychological damage.

No one ever got to the bottom of who killed Marco's parents. It was most likely a rival family, albeit none of them owned up to it. Marco's father had hidden Marco in the bedroom closet, so Marco never got a decent look at the masked assassin's eyes either.

For a long time, Marco became wild and out of control. As he moved into his teen years, Marco became violent and at times unstable. He hated acting out of control but saw no other way.

Fortunately for Marco, he was taken under the wing of a kind, calm senior Mafia man who schooled him on how to control his overriding desire for vengeance. Had Marco not met Gio

Rosa, he likely wouldn't have made it to his eighteenth birthday, let alone had the career he'd had so far.

However, Marco had always sworn to put his desire for revenge against his parents' killer to good use. Marco knew he worked in a ruthless, emotionless world that saw death and destruction as a day-to-day occupational hazard.

So as far as Marco was concerned, the feelings of anger and hate he felt toward his parent's killer would always remind him to keep a cool head and take enemies out with an emotionless accuracy.

Marco resolved to not let Aleksei's taunts get into his head any longer.

From now on, Aleksei could talk as much shit as he wanted. Marco was going to focus on the one thing he could control, and that was himself.

But training was done for the day.

With the whiskey bar in his sights, it was time for Marco to refocus his mind. It was time to down some shots with some of the best god damned Mafia Daddies in town.

Chapter 3

Rex

There was no denying it, Rex was having fun with a capital F. The surroundings may have been new to Rex, but he was definitely being shown a wild, party-loving side of the city by Kash and his gang.

'Check this out,' Kash said, popping open another bottle of highly expensive champagne and fizzing the drink up and spraying it across the cordoned off VIP section of *Dark Dreams Bar*. 'Another bottle! Let's go!'

'Woo! Woo!' Rex said, smiling, but something else slowly dawning on him.

Rex took a moment to compose himself.

As Rex looked around the plush surroundings of *Dark Dreams Bar*, he realized that while Kash and his men may have been enjoying themselves, the same probably wasn't true for the bar staff or some of the other patrons.

I don't know about this...

Kash is loud and fun, but...

This isn't the best behavior...

Rex always wanted to have fun and push things to the limits, but while doing this he was always keen to be respectful to others. The last thing that Rex would ever do would be to intentionally make anyone feel uncomfortable, and that was certainly what Kash seemed to be doing right at that moment.

Dark Dreams Bar was nice though. There was no denying that. With its crushed velvet seats and perfectly stylish chandeliers and dark furnishings, it really gave off an old school vibe.

This wasn't the kind of place that Rex would ever think to come to himself or with his other Little friends. It was far too expensive for his modest budget.

As increasingly uncomfortable as Kash's boorish behavior was making Rex feel, Rex couldn't deny that he was enjoying sipping on the five hundred dollar a bottle champagne. Although that being said, it could have done with a couple of ripe berries dropped in to sweeten the flavor a touch...

'This is nice, but I might have a juice next,' Rex said, struggling to make himself heard over the sound of Kash and his men laughing and bantering together. 'I... I... think I might ask the bartender for some juice now, actually.'

'No, allow me!' Kash replied, a menacing grin on his face as he wrapped his arm tightly around Rex. 'Bar boy! Bar boy! Over here! Right this fucking second!'

Rex cringed with embarrassment. Kash was being downright rude now. This wasn't nice behavior at all. And Rex really didn't want to be associated with it.

'I'm sorry,' Rex said, addressing the bartender as he approached Kash's table. 'I was just going to ask for a juice.'

'Yes, sir,' the bartender replied, his eyes nervously darting back and forth to Kash. 'Anything else for the table?'

'Bring me a steak,' Kash bellowed. 'And hurry the hell up! Idiot!'

The bartender looked crestfallen, but he was clearly too scared to say or do anything about how rude Kash was being.

Rex felt like suddenly all the fun had gone out of the situation. It felt like it was time to leave. At first it had been fun and exciting to hang out with Kash, but now the whole atmosphere was different.

'I... I... I think it's time for me to bounce,' Rex said, his voice trembling a little as he watched one of Kash's men pick up a handful of roasted peanuts and throw them across the bar toward a couple enjoying their meal. 'This... isn't really my thing.'

'Shut your mouth, boy,' Kash said, sneering. 'Unless you want trouble, you'll just sit there and look all cute for me. Ain't that right men?'

Kash's gang of associates all cheered raucously, and Rex felt very uncomfortable. This was in danger of turning very sour. The only question in Rex's mind was how he was going to extract himself as quickly and painlessly as possible.

'I'm just... going to the bathroom,' Rex said, trying his best to sound as casual and calm as he could.

'Stay *here*,' Kash said, pushing Rex down with one hand as he attempted to stand.

Rex knew he had to get out of there. Kash's demeanor had turned even more sour and in that moment *Dark Dream Bar* was the last place on earth that Rex wanted to be.

'Hey, bartender, where the fuck is my steak?' Kash shouted, tossing roasted peanuts in the direction of the bar, much to the amusement of his collection of thuggish friends. 'Bring it over in two minutes or I'll come into the kitchen and kick all of your asses myself.'

Rex had heard enough.

It was time to move.

Rex jumped up onto the table and scurried across it, desperate to keep his balance. Rex's entire body was being supercharged by adrenalin, and he scanned across the room to locate the quickest exit.

But just as Rex was about to get out, he felt a thud on the back of his head.

'*Urgh*. What the...?' Rex said, as he staggered toward the green EXIT sign. 'Hey, get off me!'

Before he knew what was going on, Rex was being hauled out of the VIP room by Kash and his men.

'Please, don't hurt me!' Rex cried out, punches and kicks coming down on him and he pleaded for mercy. '*Awwwww*! That hurts!'

'*Pffft*. It's less fun when they cry so quickly,' Kash said, a wicked sneer in his words. 'Let's dangle him off the edge of the balcony. That might help us work up an appetite for our bloody steaks.'

'No!' Rex squealed, terror in his voice and running through his mind too.

Rex was helpless as the thugs picked him up and carried him onto the balcony area and dangled him off the side. Rex didn't know whether they were going to drop him, and it felt like his entire life was quite literally hanging by a thread.

'I'm begging you, please!' Rex cried out, barely able to speak through fear.

'Put him down,' Kash said. 'He's had enough.'

Rex let out a sigh of relief, but if he thought Kash was done with him, he was wrong...

'Now let's beat his ass some more,' Kash cackled. 'Except this time, no holding back!'

Rex knew that he had to escape. Kash was clearly totally wild and out of control – and not in any kind of good way either.

It felt like a living, waking nightmare, but before the men could really start to beat on Rex again, he wriggled free and made a dash for the fire exit.

Keep running.

Don't look back.

I just have to... get out of here...

As Rex made his way down the emergency fire exit staircase, he could hear Kash bellowing angrily in the distance. By the sounds of it, Kash wasn't done with him. Not by a long shot.

'Don't think this is over, boy!' Kash growled, his voice carrying down the stairs toward where a breathless Rex stood. 'Come back and face more punishment. Or don't. Either way I'll make sure you pay! And when you least expect it too! You'll never be safe as long as I'm on the streets!'

With that, Rex watched as Kash slammed the fire exit door shut.

It was over. For now. But all Rex could hear were Kash's words ringing in his ears. Rex wouldn't be safe for as long as Kash was on the loose. Rex knew all about people like Kash, but he never expected to be one of his victims.

'I... need... to get home,' Rex said, his voice breaking up and tears forming in his eyes. 'I just need to feel safe again.'

Rex's apartment was his home and the place where he felt safest of all. Except today, something was different. After escaping Kash and his gang of horrible friends, Rex had made a beeline back to his apartment and after triple-locking the door was now safely wrapped underneath a blanket on the couch.

With his cherished stuffie Ozzy being gripped tight, Rex was doing his best to calm down and feel at least a little bit more at peace.

'Ozzy, that was horrible,' Rex said, picking up an apple and pear juice box and taking a long sip. 'And my tummy hurts from where they kicked me too. And my head.'

Ozzy stared back at Rex with his loving eyes and big, bushy eyebrows.

Rex simply held Ozzy tighter.

Rex looked around his apartment. It was compact, but had everything a Little could need.

There was a small bedroom that was big enough for a bed, tiny walk-in closet, and a little desk. In the living area Rex had a cozy old couch, a TV, and the rest of the space was a devoted play area where Rex was able to color, paint, play with his wooden toys, or simply lie on the comfy mat and listen to music.

But no matter how much Rex tried, not even his home comforts were taking his mind off Kash. It was one thing having had a bad experience and being beat up a little, and Rex knew he would get over that soon enough.

No, what was truly troubling Rex was Kash's threat that this wasn't over, and he would surprise him again. In fact, the thought of ever seeing Kash again was enough to make Rex want to puke.

I was so silly for ever trusting Kash.

I wanted fun, not trouble.

And now what am I meant to do?

Rex let out a long sigh. Fortunately for Rex, two of his best Little friends arrived moments later and brought with them some supplies.

Extra-cheesy pizza? Check.

Candy by the bucket-load? Check again.

A heap of positive vibes and cuddles? All the way!

'Thanks for coming guys,' Rex said, having now changed into a onesie along with his friends, Mac and Eddie. 'I really needed some company.'

'Of course we came!' Eddie said, his kind hazel eyes full of love. 'We've always got one another's backs.'

'We sure do,' Mac added, his blonde hair flopping around as he spoke. 'This Kash dude sounds like the stinkiest butt-breath ever.'

The three Littles giggled. It was a horrible situation for Rex to be in, but laughter was the best medicine. Rex always tried to see the positive side of things, or at least the humorous. With his two good friends alongside him, Rex was determined to break out of his funk.

However, thoughts of Kash and what he might do in the future were hard to ignore.

'I'm scared he might just show up,' Rex said. 'He knows where I work. What if shows up at the Peachy Playpen? Or follows me home?'

'He sounds like a bully,' Mac replied, his bright blue eyes offering a sense of hope. 'And bullies are usually cowards deep down. Isn't that right, Eddie?'

'*Hmmm*. It can be,' Mac said, a hint of caution in his voice. 'But maybe we should speak to our Daddies about this. They'd know what to do! I mean, given what they do for work...'

'Okay, let me think about it,' Rex said, still unsure but not wanting to waste any more time thinking about Kash. 'How about... a race to Littlespace?'

'Only if you think you're up to it?' Mac said, smiling kindly. 'Don't think you have to force yourself to have fun. We can just chill quietly with a movie if you want?'

'Yeah, it's up to you,' Eddie added, putting his arm around Rex. 'Whatever you want to do is golden with us.'

'Well... I want Littlespace!' Rex said, putting his bravest face on and stomping his foot for comic effect.

The three friends giggled and finished off their pizza before heading over toward the play area. As the three of them lay on the floor and began to color and sing along to the music coming from Rex's portable speaker, the atmosphere slowly but surely changed.

Soon, all three of them were regressing back and having a great time. Rex felt innocent and full of wonder as he drew a big, shiny sun and a forest and lake beneath it.

'Hey, look, I'm going to draw us all swimming with no clothes on!' Rex giggled, much to the amusement of his Little friends.

'Don't do anything too rude!' Mac giggled. 'My Daddy spanks my butt if I ever draw naked without asking!'

The Littles all rolled around laughing together.

As far as Rex was concerned, it felt good to feel more relaxed and carefree after what had happened earlier on. And the longer he was in Littlespace, the better Rex felt about his prospects of not seeing Kash again in the future.

It felt like being in Littlespace was a real escape.

But sadly, Rex couldn't stay in Littlespace for ever.

As Mac and Eddie went home to their Daddies, Rex was left alone and wondering if he could ever truly forget about Kash, and the threat that Kash might still pose to his safety?

Mac and Eddie were lucky to have deadly, ruthless Daddies who would look after them with every last bullet they could fire and every last punch they could throw. But Rex didn't have a protector like that. If Rex was ever going to see Kash again, he would have to somehow hope he was strong enough on his own...

Chapter 4

Marco

A couple of weeks passed and training at the MMA gym was as intense as ever. As the tournament grew closer, Marco was stepping up his efforts and pushing his body like never before.

The shadow of Aleksei may have still been lurking at most training sessions, but Marco was adept at keeping his distance and not giving Aleksei a reason to start firing off his stupid insults and trash-talking.

Marco may have been a ruthless and often violent criminal, but he had been trained well enough to know that sometimes the best way of handling an opponent was by not giving them oxygen to thrive on – and that form of oxygen in Aleksei's case being Marco's attention.

Marco's approach seemed to be working too.

From what Marco was hearing from the other guys in the gym, Aleksei had been skipping sessions and not quite putting in the same ferocious effort as he was renowned for.

Perhaps Aleksei was so confident about beating Marco that he felt he could cut corners? If he was taking this approach, then Marco felt like half the battle was already won.

Marco knew from countless bank heists that mistakes happened and people were either fatally shot or arrested when they got sloppy with their preparation.

Marco would never let a detail slide when he was plotting a robbery, and he was determined to take this exact approach when it came to the fight with Aleksei too.

It was true that Aleksei had size and youth on his side, but increasingly Marco was feeling confident that he had the superior mentality and attitude. And those two factors counted as much as, if not more than, pretty much anything else.

Another strategy that Marco knew to lean on was to compartmentalize. So rather than thinking of the fight the whole time, Marco was making the most of a rare opportunity to socialize with his fellow Daddy friends.

After doing some early morning planning on a bank job, Marco was feeling fresh and clear-minded as he arrived at the *Peachy Playpen* to meet up with Dante and Rocco.

Marco was wearing his customary tailored shirt, but had paired it with some slightly more casual but still super-chic chinos. He wasn't exactly a regular at the Peachy Playpen, so wasn't entirely sure whether he was still too formally dressed.

Fortunately for Marco, he had his Daddy friends to set him right…

'Brother, you look superb,' Rocco said, arching his eyebrow and shaking Marco's hand firmly. 'I mean... you do realize they won't have table service here, right?'

'*Grrrr*. Very good, bring the jokes,' Marco said, unbuttoning an extra button on his shirt to at least try to look more casual.

'Marco, you look great,' Dante said, embracing Marco. 'We've got a round of doppios on the way. It's not exactly the primo coffee we normally have, but it's not total shit either.'

The three men laughed and took their seats around the special Daddy table that was slightly set back from the Littles as they charged around and had what looked like the time of their lives.

'Mac, be careful!' Dante hollered, noticing that Mac was attempting to balance a big mug of apple juice on his head. 'You're already on a yellow warning. One more and it's red!'

'Y-y-y-yes, Daddy,' Mac replied, giggling and blushing as he took the mug off his head and returned to cavorting with his friends.

'Yellow warning?' Marco said curious as to what this meant.

'Yellow means a hand spanking later,' Dante said, a wicked grin on his face. 'Red means... the paddle.'

'I see,' Marco replied, sipping on his freshly delivered and piping hot doppio. 'Damn. You guys have it *good*.'

'So could you,' Rocco said, finishing his coffee and signaling for another. 'You just need to find the one boy you connect with. When you know, you know. You know?'

Marco nodded.

It was good to see just how happy Dante and Rocco were with their boys. It genuinely filled Marco's heart with happiness to see two of his oldest friends in the business finding true love with a pair of great boys.

I'm happy for Marco and Dante.

They deserve it more than anyone.

I just wish that I had what they have...

Marco then saw that Rocco was returning from the café area with a plate full of the creamiest looking cakes. There were cupcakes, swirly-creams, and cookies loaded with the whitest frosting imaginable.

'These aren't for us, right?' Marco said, disdainfully.

'Relax man,' Dante said. 'I know we're Daddies, but that doesn't mean we can't indulge in some Little treats from time to time.'

'For sure,' Rocco said, adding his two cents. 'If I'm up late and Eddie is fast asleep in bed, I'll sneak into his treat cupboard in the kitchen and grab a quick handful of candys for myself!'

Rocco and Dante high-fived one another, but Marco was less than impressed.

'I'll pass, guys,' Marco said. 'My pre-fight diet is too strict to go wasting calories like that. Hmph. Maybe the single life suits me better.'

But as Marco watched Rocco and Dante scoffing the cakes, Marco couldn't help but notice a boy over on the reception desk.

He's cute as hell.

But he looks so sad. Almost... scared?

Maybe he needs a sugary snack...

With that, Marco grabbed a small selection of cupcakes and put them on a paper plate before walking over toward the reception desk.

As Marco got closer, he found himself totally blown away by the boy. He was undeniably cute, and despite looking under the weather he had a hint of mischief about him.

Physically, the boy was exactly what Marco looked for. Slender, athletic, and with just a hint of muscle on his arms.

But Marco couldn't spend all day staring. He was now standing directly in front of the boy with a plate of food in his hands...

'Um, can I help you?' the boy said. 'My name's Rex, I'm on reception today. Anything you need, just ask.'

'Well, it was more what I could do for you,' Marco said, handing the plate over. 'I hope you don't mind me saying, but you looked like you could do with some cheering up.'

There was a pause as Rex eyed up the plate of food.

For a moment, Marco wasn't sure whether he'd crossed a line. After all, he may have been a Daddy Dom, but Rex was a member of staff at the *Peachy Playpen*, it might not have been entirely appropriate to approach him like this.

'Sorry, I stepped over the mark,' Marco said, feeling disappointed that his advance had seemingly been rebuffed. 'Please forgive me.'

'No! No! Thank you,' Rex said, his voice all over the place but a smile breaking out. 'I was miles away. I've had a rough couple of weeks to tell you the truth. Sorry, I didn't catch your name?'

'That's because I didn't say it. Force of habit, I guess,' Marco replied. 'But it's Santino. Marco Santino. I'm here with Rocco and Dante.'

'Ah, I see, yeah,' Rex said, his face lighting up. 'I'm friends with their Littles, Eddie and Mac. Oh, so you must be...'

'I'm in the same line of work as Rocco and Dante, yes, that's right,' Marco said, making it clear that he wasn't about to go into any unnecessary details. 'But tell me about you. Something's clearly eating you up inside. You can trust me, I'm good when it comes to this kind of thing.'

Marco could see and feel that Rex needed his help.

It may have been instinct, but every bone in Marco's body was telling him that this boy needed his assistance. It might have been a small problem, or something a whole lot bigger. Marco didn't know either way. But one thing that Marco knew for absolute certain was that Rex needed to get it off his chest.

There's something up.

I know that look on his face.

And I know that I'm the man he needs to help him...

It didn't take long before Rex started to open up. And in truth, it was way worse than Marco could have imagined...

'So you're saying that this... Kash Vialli... beat you, threatened you, and is still after you?' Marco said, barely able to believe that someone would be so cruel to a boy as sweet and genuine as Rex. 'I can't allow this.'

'But... you don't know me?' Rex said, clearly emotional. 'I couldn't ask that of you. And anyway, it doesn't matter what you say to Kash. He wants to kill me, I know he does. I even heard that he's been going to Little clubs across the city and telling other Littles that I'm on his hit list. At first I thought it was a cruel game, but now I'm convinced he means it!'

'Boy, calm down,' Marco said, a little abruptly. 'You need to breathe. Take a moment. Focus. You won't make this better by letting your emotions run away with you.'

Marco's words seemed to work.

Rex took a moment to compose himself. But it was clear as Rex continued to explain the situation that Kash Vialli was a loose cannon, and a twisted, evil one at that.

Marco was beginning to realize that this wasn't going to simply be a case of giving the boy some advice and then walking away. This was something altogether bigger. And it would require more work on his part too.

'He's just a big, bad bully,' Rex said, his eyes filling with tears again. 'I used to have so much fun. Now I'm scared to leave my apartment. I'm even scared when I'm in there!'

The moment got too much for Rex and before Marco could stop him, Rex had burst past him and ran into the bathroom.

Suddenly, Marco was joined by both Dante and Rocco.

'Looks intense,' Dante said. 'This wouldn't by any chance be about Kash Vialli would it?'

'Yup,' Marco replied.

'Hell no,' Rocco said. 'I'd heard about him from Eddie but hadn't had time to find out more. You know how busy things have been. I honestly didn't realize it was so serious.'

The three Daddies looked at one another.

'I fucking hate bullies,' Marco growled. 'And I hate to see a boy like Rex suffer. I'm going to put an end to Kash Vialli. Scum like him don't deserve to be walking the streets. Don't worry guys, I've got this.'

Dante and Rocco nodded in approval.

Marco thought back to how helpless and distraught he felt as a child when his mother and father were assassinated. Being so small and young meant he hadn't been able to do anything but watch on as his parents were murdered. Feeling powerless was the worst feeling in the world, and it was exactly how Marco imagined Rex was feeling with regards to Kash Vialli and his gang.

Marco was determined to set this situation right for Rex. However before he could do that, he needed more information, and he needed it *right now*...

Chapter 5

Rex

Rex was trying as best as he could to compose himself in the bathroom. With tears flowing down his cheeks faster than he could wipe them away, it wasn't easy.

'Come on, you've got this,' Rex said, his bottom lip trembling.

As far as Rex was concerned, talking about Kash had simply made things a whole heap worse. It was hard enough to get through a shift at the Peachy Playpen without constantly worrying about whether Kash and his men might make a reappearance.

It was clear that Marco meant well with his words, but unfortunately it had felt like the more Marco spoke, the more real the Kash situation became. In truth, what Rex really wanted more than anything was to forget that Kash ever existed.

If I could just wipe Kash off the face of the earth...

If I could magic him away and never see him again.

Who am I kidding?

Rex wiped away some more tears and splashed his face with water from the bathroom tap. The feeling of the cold water on his red face did serve to calm Rex down a little bit.

However, it also served to sharpen Rex's thoughts. The truth was that ever since the incident with Kash, Rex hadn't been the same. The cuts and bruises had healed well enough, but the emotional distress of the situation was still all too raw.

Rex had gone from a carefree, fun-loving risk-taker to someone living within themselves. Smiling was hard, and laughter felt like a thing of the past.

'I just want to have some *fun* again,' Rex said, looking at himself in the mirror. 'I just want Kash to go away so I can get on with my life.'

Rex sighed.

Knowing that Kash could be around any corner, or waiting for Rex at his apartment building, was too much stress to live with. It had crossed Rex's mind that he could leave his beloved *Peach Playpen* and get a job somewhere else. Rex could also leave New York City and start afresh somewhere else.

But Rex didn't want to do *either* of these things.

It seemed so unfair that Kash got to act like a violent bully and get away with it, while his victims had to struggle on in life as if nothing had happened.

At one point, Rex had considered going to the police. But he knew this was a bad idea. Men like Kash didn't care what the police thought, and Rex was certain that Kash would come fully loaded with the most expensive, devious lawyer in the whole city.

No, if Rex was going to get Kash out of his life he would need to take some drastic action. The only question was exactly what that drastic action would look like?

The sound of Littles having fun outside of the bathroom brought Rex's mind back into sharp focus. Hopefully there wasn't a line of people waiting to be served at the reception desk.

Speaking of which, Rex began to wonder about Marco...

Marco Santino... bad guy? Good guy? Daddy?

He's handsome. Older. Commanding.

But what does he want from me?

Now that he thought of it, Rex had heard the name Marco Santino being bandied about by Eddie and Mac's Daddies. Marco was a good friend of theirs, and Rex had heard snapshots of conversations where Marco was the subject.

Marco had a reputation for cold, clinical violence. He was a bank robber. A man not to be crossed under any circumstances.

All of this should have sent a shiver of fear up and down Rex's body. Except, it didn't. In fact, Rex couldn't decide how he felt about Marco. They had only just met, and not exactly in ideal circumstances either. But there was something there between them. It was hard for Rex to say what it was, but there was a connection.

'*Pfft*! Stop being silly!' Rex said, by way of snapping himself out of any kind of romantic or lustful thoughts about Marco. 'I'm trying to escape a bad man, the *last* thing I need is another entering my life...'

Rex dried off his face and took a big gulp of air. He knew it was more than time for him to get back out there and face the world.

But before Rex left the bathroom, he thought back to his father. Rex's father's dying wish had been that he enjoyed his life and never took anything *too* seriously.

Rex had happily gone along with that mantra and was grateful that his father had given him such a wholesome, positive way of thinking to live by. However after what had happened with Kash, Rex was no longer sure whether he was going to live by his father's words. And this might just have been the saddest thing of all.

'Come on, don't get all emotional again,' Rex said, standing tall and focusing his mind. 'It's time to be a big boy and go back out there. If I don't show my face soon, I might not have a job to go back to at all.'

With that, Rex opened the door and stepped out into the Peachy Playpen. However, before he could get to the reception desk, there was someone waiting for him, and they looked like they meant serious business...

* * *

'Marco?' Rex said, unsure what to make of Marco having clearly waited for him to exit the bathroom. 'What's... um... I need to get back to the reception desk.'

Rex waited for Marco to respond.

But all Marco did was shake his head and put his arm around Rex's shoulder. This should have shocked Rex, made him move away, or even tell Marco to get off him.

But it felt right.

Suddenly, Rex felt safe. It was uncanny, but simply having Marco put his arm gently around his shoulder made the whole world seem like a safe place again. However as good as it felt, Rex needed to hear what Marco's thoughts were at some point...

'Am... am I in trouble?' Rex said.

'No, boy, you're not,' Marco replied, his dark brown eyes looking kind and soulful as they stared at Rex. 'Not anymore.'

'I don't get it,' Rex replied, his mind running wild with possibilities as to exactly what Marco meant.

'Well allow me to explain,' Marco said, his voice low and serious, but with an edge of kindness to it. 'I've spoken to your boss and he's says it's okay for you to have some time off. Your job is safe. But I need to keep you out of here until this Kash Vialli situation is cleared up.'

'W-w-what?' Rex replied. 'Are you serious?'

'I am, but there's a condition,' Marco continued. 'You'll need to move in with me, just until the situation is done with. I'll take Kash and his men out. You'll never have to worry about those low-life vermin again. But under my roof, you'll have to follow my rules. Understood? And I mean *all* my rules.'

'All of your rules?' Rex said, intrigued, excited and a little bit unsure too. 'I don't know what *any* of your rules are!'

'Everything will be agreed upon. It will all be above board and legit,' Marco said, his voice firm and reassuring. 'But when all is said and done, if you agree to this then you will be my boy, and everything that comes with that.'

Rex's heart was beating in triple-time.

This sounded almost too good to be true.

Marco was offering to get rid of Kash and remove the one thing that was making Rex's life a misery. At the same time, there was an offer for Rex to live as Marco's boy for the duration of however long it took for Marco to remove Kash.

This is a no-brainer.

There must be a catch, something I'm missing.

It might be a risk to say yes, but...

'Okay, I agree,' Rex said, his voice wavering a little bit.

'*Okay?* That doesn't sound like you're very sure,' Marco said. 'I need to hear some enthusiastic consent. The last thing I want to do is get you involved in something where you're not sure you want to do it. I'm not like the Kash Vialli's of this world. I'm cut from a totally different cloth, that's for damn sure.'

'No, I mean super-yes!' Rex said, his voice still trembling with excitement. 'I was just nervous, is all. I really, really, *really* want to do this.'

Marco smiled and held out his hand for Rex to shake.

Rex's heartrate was still sky-high, and adrenalin was pumping around his body faster than he could even begin to comprehend. This was a risk, that was for sure. Rex knew that he barely knew Marco, and on the basis of what happened with Kash, that was hardly a good omen.

But Marco was so clearly different to Kash.

No, this felt like it was the right thing to do. With Kash and his gang on the loose, Rex didn't know whether there was a single better option on the table for him.

All that Marco knew was that with his delicate hand safely inside the clasp Marco's big, powerful hand, suddenly Kash seemed far less of a threat to him.

'Come on, boy,' Marco said. 'It's time I showed you where you'll be living, for now at least. We'll stop off for some supplies on the way, but the sooner we get you home to my place, the better. You need some good, old-fashioned care and attention to get you feeling yourself again. And without doubt, I'm the man to do it.

'Y-y-yes, Marco,' Rex said, resisting the urge to call him Daddy. 'I can't wait.'

This felt like a big moment to Rex.

Perhaps it was the biggest moment for Rex in some time, his whole life even. Either way, it was time to say goodbye to the *Peachy Playpen* for now and head out with his new protector and avenger, Marco.

'See you soon, *Peachy*!' Rex said, turning his head one final time as they left through the front door. 'Hopefully I'll be back again soon...'

Chapter 6

Marco

The journey from the Peachy Playpen back to Marco's apartment was as smooth as Marco could have hoped for. After stopping quickly at a bodega to pick up some fruit and vegetables, plus one of Rex's favorite breakfast cereals, Marco and his new boy were pulling up outside of his apartment building.

'You have someone who parks your car for you?' Rex said, awe in his voice. 'Wow! I don't think my building even has a carpark.'

'Ha. Well, yeah. This place is a bit on the fancy side, I guess,' Marco said, now having grown used to the luxury of this part of his life. 'The doormen here are good guys. You can trust them. If you ever need something and I'm not around, they're a safe bet.'

Rex nodded and Marco could see that this was indeed quite a big deal for Rex. On the way over from the *Peachy Playpen*, they had both given potted histories of their past relationships and Rex didn't have much experience. Rex was young and didn't have as much life experience – which was to be expected given his age of course.

I'm going to have to be careful.

The boy is fragile. He's been through a lot.

But he's got character, a spirit that needs to be encouraged...

After handing the car over to the valet, Marco and Rex entered the main lobby and judging by the look on Rex's face, he was seriously impressed. With its marble floor and paneled walls, the lobby was a throwback to old New York, the kind that Rex would only have known from the movies.

'Don't worry kid, this was all strange and new to me once too,' Marco said as the pair of them stepped into the gold lined elevator. 'My old man may have been involved in the business, but he never had a lot of money. We grew up humble. But we were happy too, until...'

'Until?' Rex said, an inquisitive tone in his voice as he ran his fingers over the elevator buttons, careful not to press on them too hard.

'A story for another time, perhaps,' Marco said, shutting the conversation down. 'We need to look to the future. I've got a feeling that everything is going to work out for you, I really do. And I've always been known for my intuition. It's part of the reason for how I've lasted so long in the game.'

'And what's the other part?' Rex replied.

'Planning. Lots and lots of planning,' Marco chuckled. 'I'm a big believer that you make your own luck. The amount of young up and comers who score a few lucky jobs and then either get their bellies filled with lead or end up serving forty-year sentences tells me everything I need to know. The second you get cocky and stop putting the work in, that's when you'll be caught out. But, enough about my work. Let's talk about you.'

'What do you want to know?' Rex said, giggling mischievously as the elevator door pinged and opened on the penthouse level. 'Too late!'

With that, Rex ran ahead and made his way to the door to Marco's apartment. Marco wasn't impressed with Rex's sass, but on the other hand it was good to see the boy relaxing and little and letting his fun side come to the fore.

'You can't run from me!' Marco bellowed. 'I want answers, and I'll get them soon enough.'

With a huge smile on his face, Marco ran after Rex and caught up with him at the door to his apartment. For a brief moment, there was a flash of electricity between Marco and Rex as they stood in the doorway together.

Certainly, Marco was struggling to control his instincts...

I want to kiss him.

Those lips. Those eyes. That damn strawberry earring.

He's the sexiest boy I've ever...

But before Marco could give in to his animalistic desires, he composed himself and opened the apartment door.

'Inside, let's go,' Marco said, trying his best to sound as formal and austere as he could. 'I'll show you where your room is.'

'Woah, this place is… *big*,' Rex said, immediately making himself feel at home as he wandered from room to room, inspecting it all and taking in as much as he possibly could.

Marco couldn't help but smile as he saw the youthful exuberance and excitement flow from Rex's every pore. Marco was in his mid-forties and had seen far too much death and destruction in his life to personally get excited about much, but being able to live vicariously through Rex for a moment was a total joy.

However, that wasn't to say that everything would be plain sailing in their living arrangement…

'Boy! Be careful!' Marco barked, the sight of Rex nearly crashing into a priceless Italian vase nearly sending Marco into a world of pain. 'Have fun but keep those damned eyes on where' you're going.'

'*Ooops*, sorry!' Rex replied, a little too casually for Marco's liking.

Marco could see that Rex was going to be a pleasure to live with. He was also going to be a boy that would need discipline too, that much was obvious and he'd only been at Marco's place for less than ten minutes.

Whatever happened next, Marco knew that it was going to present a different challenge to his usual day of Mafia business and plotting bank heists.

A challenge it might be to have Rex under his roof for the duration of the Kash situation, but Marco had a feeling that he was going to relish every single moment of it…

* * *

As soon as Rex had unpacked his stuff, Marco decided that the pair of them would head across the road to *Mini's Bistro*, a quiet little restaurant and bar that Marco enjoyed.

Marco held the door to *Mini's* open for Rex and smiled as he watched the boy enter ahead of him. There was something so sweet about Rex's open-eyed innocence and clear enjoyment of experiencing new things.

Just like he had felt back at the apartment, Marco was enjoying being in the company of someone who didn't have a jaded, seen-it-all-before approach to life.

'Your usual table, sir?' the maître d', said.

'Yes, that would be fantastic, Giles,' Marco replied, smiling at Rex as the pair of them were led over to a quiet table in the corner of the bistro.

'I like sitting here,' Marco said. 'It may not be as fancy as a big window seat, but it lets me see everything that's going on. You may have already guessed, but I like to be in control.'

'*Yup*, the thought had definitely crossed my mind,' Rex said, a flash of mischief in his emerald, green eyes. 'The menu looks big. And I don't know what a lot of these dishes are. Would you... maybe... help me choose?'

'Of course, boy,' Marco replied, beaming with pride that Rex had shown that trust in him. 'You never need to be shy about asking for my help. That's what I'm here for. I *want* to look after you. I *want* to protect you.'

Rex blushed and buried his head behind the large, expensively bound menu. Marco couldn't help but chuckle. Rex certainly had a mischievous and carefree side to him, but he was tender and shy too at times. It made for quite the combination.

By the time the food and drinks arrived at the table a few minutes later, the conversation between the two of them was in full flow.

Marco was enjoying listening to Rex talk all about his life working at the Peachy Playpen, and about all of the fun and games he enjoyed getting up to with his fellow Little friends.

Listening to Rex, it all sounded so wonderful and idyllic to Marco.

And it made Marco *even more* determined to avenge Rex and take Kash out of the picture forever.

'And one time,' Rex said, picking up the water jug carelessly. 'One time... I ate so many candies that I thought my pee-pee was going to turn rainbow colored. OMG! No!'

'Boy!' Marco growled, the water from the larger water jug spilling onto the table and down onto the floor too. 'I told you to be careful. But you didn't listen.'

'Chill, it's just water,' Rex said, seemingly finding it all very amusing.

'Enough!' Marco said, his tone of voice suddenly far more severe. 'An accident is one thing, but not owning your mistake is another. And even worse is adopting a flippant attitude in the aftermath. Now go to the bathroom and clean yourself up. And as you're drying your pants, you can think of a safeword.'

'A safeword?' Rex said, the laughter and giggling replaced by a look of shock. 'As in... an actual safeword?'

'You've got it,' Marco replied. 'You might be needing it sooner than you'd imagined.'

With that, Rex scurried off to the bathroom.

Marco was feeling charged up and could easily have bent Rex over the dining table right there and then and tanned his bare bottom. But this was about to be Rex's first spanking, and it needed to be in the safe and secure confines of Marco's apartment.

Marco felt the blood pumping around his body.

If this boy thinks he can publicly sass me, he's got another thing coming.

We're going to start as we mean to go along.

Those round little cheeks won't know what's hit them...

Having walked back from *Mini's Bistro* in silence, Marco was determined to make things crystal clear to Rex. Yes, he was helping the boy to overcome Kash and be able to live his life freely and with fun again. But on the other hand, respect was respect... and Marco expected to be treated like the true Mafia Daddy he was.

'It was j-j-just some water,' Rex said, even then a hint of a smile on his face as they entered Marco's penthouse. 'I mean... it wasn't like it was a three-hundred-dollar bottle of wine, right?'

Marco remained silent.

Rex may have been a cocky, bratty little boy in that moment, but Marco was going to handle him like he would any rival. Sometimes silence could be more powerful than words. And so it proved to be with Rex too.

'Water? It doesn't stain,' Rex said, slightly more apprehensively as Marco continued to keep his mouth shut. 'And I did kind of offer to clean it up...'

Marco considered breaking his silence, but he wanted to see how long Rex would go before breaking.

Keep talking boy.

Are you going to make it worse for yourself?

Do you think you can talk me out of this spanking, huh?

Rex continued to talk, making wilder and wilder statements as he looked for a way out of what he surely knew was going to be a strictly administered spanking headed his way.

'The table was wobbly! It wasn't my fault the jug slipped,' Rex said, blushing and not even able to maintain eye contact with Marco.

Marco walked into the large open-plan kitchen and took a seat on one of the heavy wooden chairs. He spread his legs a little and felt his throbbing dick push and strain inside his pants.

'It's time, boy,' Marco said. 'And to confirm... your safeword is?'

'It's yogurt,' Rex said, a sudden air of resignation in his voice. 'My safeword is yogurt.'

'Good, now come over here and stand before me,' Marco said, his voice clear and calm. 'I want you to pull your jeans down and put your hands on your head for me. I won't ask twice.'

Marco watched as Rex submitted himself to his commands.

Fuck. I want to take him right here and now.

But this isn't about sex, no matter how much I might want that.

This is about teaching the boy a lesson.

'I'm going to pull these sweet little yellow briefs down to your knees and I'm then going to bend you over my lap,' Marco said, his heart thumping and his eyes drawn to the sight of Rex's hard cock springing up as he pulled the tight yellow briefs down. 'Now, over my lap.'

Marco felt Rex gasp as he bent him over. The sight of Rex's stiff cock had done nothing but further excite Marco, and he could feel his own manhood throbbing even harder.

But this was a spanking.

It wasn't a prelude to *anything* else.

This was a punishment, and it was going to be carried out properly...

'You will take six spanks on each cheek, boy,' Marco said. 'You will thank me after each one. If, and only if, I am satisfied, we will call it there.'

'Y-y-y-yes, D....' Rex said. 'Yes, Mr. Santino, sir.'

Marco rubbed the flat of his hand over Rex's pale, perfectly presented ass cheeks as a means of warming them up just a touch. This was going to be a stern spanking, and Marco wanted to give Rex the best chance of making it through all the way.

'Can I just say one thing?' Rex said, his voice full of nerves.

'Quickly,' Marco said, suspecting that Rex might be stalling for time.

'I think I deserve this,' Rex said. 'Please, give me the spanking I *need*.'

'I certainly will, don't worry about that,' Marco replied, pleased to hear that Rex was owning the moment, but also cautious that Rex wasn't trying to curry favor with him either in the hope of an easier spanking. 'Let's get to it then.'

THWACK!

THWACK!

THWACK!

THWACK!

THWACK!

THWACK!

'*Awwww*! It stings, it stings! I mean, thank you Mr. Santino,' Rex said, his body wriggling around on Marco's wide, strong lap.

'That's a good three spanks on each cheek,' Marco said. 'We're halfway there. Now let's not waste another second. You're doing well. But this next six will be *harder*.'

Marco wasn't lying either. The final six spanks, three on each cheek, were considerably firmer and the loud cracking noise each one made was a testament to that.

Marco could tell that Rex was close to the edge of what he could handle, but it was also clear that Rex was determined to hold on and take his punishment in full. That was a good sign, and it made Marco determined to deliver absolutely the most spot-on, butt-roastingly accurate spanks he could dish out.

'And we're done,' Marco said, immediately reaching into the cupboard behind him and taking out a pot of cooling gel. 'I think your little tush is in need of some TLC.'

'Yes, D....,' Rex said, his voice soft and calmer than Marco had heard it up until this point.

Marco began to gently work the cooling gel into Rex's hot cheeks. They were so supple, and sensitive too after taking the full force of Marco's flat hand.

Marco could feel Rex's body reacting to the cool cream as he slid and worked it between his cheeks too. But Marco knew he couldn't take this any further, no matter how much he might want to.

'It's okay, you can call me whatever you like,' Marco said. 'It's up to you. In fact, I want you to always know you can speak to me and tell me how you feel. If there's something you don't like in a spanking, I want to hear about it. This will only work if both of us are communicating.'

'Okay, I will,' Rex said. 'That was a good spanking. I don't think I've had one that felt like that before. But...'

'Yes?' Marco said, attentive to Rex's needs.

'I think I feel all sleepy now,' Rex said, turning his head to look up at Marco, his eyes full of emotion.

'I thought you might,' Marco said. 'But I don't think my maid has been in today, so I'm going to let you nap in my bed. Come on, I'll carry you through.'

'Can I have Ozzy with me too?' Rex said, snuggling up in Marco's arms as he carried him. 'I can't sleep without Ozzy.'

'Of course you can, boy,' Marco said, chuckling. 'I know how much a boy needs his stuffie.'

And moments later, Rex was tucked up in Marco's king-sized bed with his beloved stuffie, Ozzy. With the covers tucked up underneath him, Rex looked about as snuggly and ready for a nice long nap as you could ever imagine.

Marco would have *loved* to have gotten into bed with Rex too.

But now wasn't the time for that. It might never be either. All Marco knew was that he was looking after the boy and had just given him a well-earned spanking across his lap.

'Sleep well,' Marco said, closing the bedroom door. 'I've got lots of work to be getting on with, so don't worry about me. Just let those little eyes shut and I'll see you when you wake up.'

'Okay... Daddy,' Rex said, bringing Ozzy in even closer to his body and shutting his eyes.

Marco smiled and his heart filled with joy.

If this is what being a Daddy to a boy could be like, he wanted more. But before that, there was the small matter of his never-ending Mafia work to be getting on with.

I'm going to look after Rex.

Whatever it takes, I'll do it.

Kash Vialli doesn't know it, but his days are numbered...

Chapter 7

Rex

Marco's bed was comfortable in the way that Rex imagined a bed in a five-star hotel would be. It was big, like *seriously* big. The mattress was firm but had just the right amount of spring in it. And Rex could tell that the covers were made from the finest materials. All in all, it was the perfect bed to nap in.

The spanking had been an intense experience.

There was something so magical about being put across the lap of a man who really knew what he was doing with his spanking hand. Marco's grip was firm, and his spanks were hard and landed with a crisp accuracy that Rex knew wasn't as easy to achieve as many might imagine.

Oh, and the spanks *hurt* too.

But Rex loved the way that after the punishment was over, it was clear that Marco only had his best interests at heart. Actually, the way that Marco had checked in half-way through the spanking was great too. Rex appreciated Marco's attention to detail and the fact that the spanking was given with the best intentions at heart.

It hadn't been a punishment to inflict pain or to humiliate Rex, it had been a necessary lesson in discipline that Rex could see that he needed.

Rex knew full well that Marco had done plenty of bad things in his life. It was all part of the Mafia lifestyle, a total occupational hazard. It may even have been the case that Marco *enjoyed* what he did in his professional life.

That was still a scary thought for Rex, but it didn't seem to matter too much. When Rex was in Marco's company, he felt safe and secure, and none more so than when he was across Marco's lap and having his bottom warmed up something toasty.

As Rex woke up from his long, super-cozy nap, he sat up in the bed and looked around Marco's room.

'Marco's... seriously rich,' Rex said, looking down at Ozzy. 'I don't know much about the high life, but these paintings...'

Rex cast his eyes over the various paintings that hung from the walls. Rich in detail and framed in classy, ornate golden frames, the paintings were spellbinding.

'Some of these are... wild,' Rex said, blushing a little as he took in the images of naked men wrapped up in one another's bodies. 'I think I'd struggle to control myself seeing these men every night at bedtime...'

Rex recalled the sensation of lying across Marco's lap and the feeling of Marco's big bulge digging into his tummy. Rex giggled at the thought of it, and couldn't help but wonder exactly what Marco's cock would feel like, free from his pants...

No, stop thinking about it!

This is a professional arrangement.

No sex. No... naughtiness. No...

With his mind raging with possibilities and very much fighting a losing battle when it came to imagining all the things he and Marco could do to one another, Rex decided that the best option was to hop up and out of bed and find Marco.

After putting his pajama bottoms on, Rex wandered out of the bedroom and in search of Marco. The apartment was bigger than Rex had previously realized. Despite having run excitedly around it on arrival, it seemed that Rex had in fact missed a couple of side corridors and there was even a large room with nothing but a grand piano in it.

'Art, a grand piano... spankings... and guns and murder,' Rex said, whispering the words to himself. 'Who *is* this guy? Beats me.'

Rex skipped across the floor and walked into the central lobby area of the apartment. There was a handwritten note on the shiny, deep mahogany desk...

Gone out to pick some necessary items up. Back soon. Make yourself at home boy. But be careful around the vases... ;)
DADDY MARCO.

. . .

It was a thrill for Rex to see Marco describe himself like that. Even though Rex had called Marco Daddy before his nap, it still felt very new and unusual.

Is he really my Daddy?

I don't know if I'm ready...

But somehow it just feels right.

Rex put the note back down on the desk and decided it was time for a nice, steaming hot shower.

As he walked into the main bathroom and took his pajama bottoms off, Rex saw that his cock was still a little bit hard. Not exactly a full-on raging erection, but not totally soft either. It must have been the simple fact of being alone and barely dressed in Marco's apartment that was doing it, because the underlying feeling of being turned on simply wasn't going anywhere.

The sensible option at this point might have been to have an icy cold shower, but Rex decided he wanted to try another approach...

'Let's get all steamy, shall we,' Rex giggled as he turned the shower onto max heat and power and watched as the shower unit filled with a thick steam.

As Rex opened the door and stepped into the shower unit, his mind began to swirl with thoughts of Marco wearing nothing but his tiny MMA shorts.

The pair of them had discussed hobbies when they were at *Mini's Bistro*, and from the second that Marco had mentioned his, Rex's mind had been aflame with thoughts of Marco in a variety of combat and wrestling sportswear.

As the hot water cascaded over Rex, he felt his cock rise and begin to ache with desire. Rex began to run his hands down the front of his wet body and toward his erect dick.

As Rex grabbed his shaft, he imagined how it would feel for Marco's hands to be all over him, squeezing and pulling, giving pleasure in a way that only a big, stern Daddy could.

We may not be together like that.

But that doesn't mean I can't imagine what it would be like.

There are definitely no rules forbidding that...

Rex gasped as he began to work his cock harder and build into a perfect rhythm. Before long, Rex closed his eyes and felt nothing but pleasure in the steamiest shower he had probably ever taken...

The shower may have turned into something altogether hotter than Rex had imagined, but after washing himself clean and drying his body with one of the many perfectly folded fluffy white towels on offer, Rex was feeling fresh and chilled out.

The only question was what was taking Marco so long?

Rex got himself changed into some fresh clothes and decided he would make the most of his time alone and check out the impressive cinema-style projector in Marco's living space.

'I could watch cartoons... or I could try something more Marco-style,' Rex giggled, using the TV remote to scroll through the countless options.

In the end, Rex settled upon a gangster series. It was one of these new big-budget series that had it all. Action, hot guys, and lots of twists and turns.

'What's not to love!' Rex giggled, snuggling up on the large couch with Ozzy and watching in awe as the series immediately dropped Rex into a world of extreme violence and drama. 'This looks like it might be a bit scary. But... I'm a big boy, I can handle it...'

As the first episode continued at a relentless pace, Rex suddenly found himself getting more and more scared. He knew he shouldn't be watching a show like this, especially alone. There was something too close to his current reality about it for Rex to deal with and before long he was regretting even putting it on.

I should turn this off.

But... it's still kinda fun.

Even if it could give me nightmares.

As the first episode ended and the second episode automatically started playing, Rex began to have thoughts about Kash. There were baddies in the show just like him. They were mean, ruthless, and didn't care about hurting anyone if it meant they got what they wanted.

All of a sudden, Rex was feeling panicky about his situation with Kash. But not only that, Rex was thinking about Marco too. Rex didn't know whether Marco knew exactly how horrible

Kash was, and the thought of Marco getting hurt too was difficult for Rex to handle.

The second episode opened with a gruesome murder scene, and Rex nearly jumped out of his seat as he grabbed a big cushion and attempted to hide behind it.

Rex jumped again as he heard the sound of heavy bags hitting the floor. He turned around from the couch and saw Marco there. And Marco did *not* look happy. In fact, the gruff Daddy did not look happy at all.

'What the hell is going on here?' Marco said, his voice full of impatience. 'You shouldn't be watching this kind of thing alone. It's not suitable for boys to watch without their Daddies. And I know that you know that too, judging by your reaction.'

Rex didn't know what to say.

Rex could see that the shopping bags were full of what appeared to be Little supplies – diapers, pacifiers, toys, fun cereals and more.

'Are they... for me?' Rex said, his voice full of hope, his heart warmed by how sweet Marco was underneath his deadly persona.

'They are,' Marco replied. 'But we need to get some important issues ironed out first. I didn't mean to sound so angry about the gangster series. But my point was correct, you shouldn't be watching this kind of thing without checking with me. I'd be saying that even if it wasn't for your current *problems* too. Am I understood?'

'Yes, Daddy,' Rex nodded, knowing full well that Marco was right. 'I'm sorry. I messed up, I know I did. If I want to watch something a bit scary, I'll ask and watch with you instead.'

'Don't worry about it,' Marco replied. 'We all get things wrong. Me included. Now, get that butt off the couch and come and show me how to play with these wooden cars. I've got some wooden horses too, and what I think is a dinosaur. Come on, get over here right now. Daddy's orders!'

Rex quickly flicked the TV off and raced toward Marco.

As he took the toys out of the bags with a look of sheer glee on his face, Rex knew what he needed to do.

Pausing for a moment, Rex put down a perfectly crafted wooden lion and looked at Marco.

'Everything okay, boy?' Marco said, a puzzled look on his face. 'I hope I chose well. The man in the store was very helpful, but I know you boys have your personal favorites.'

'Daddy, it's all perfect,' Rex said. 'I just wanted to say thank you.'

'No problem, it's a total pleasure,' Marco smiled. 'Now, how about we set up a village where all the toys can play together?'

Rex smiled the kind of smile that could light up a thousand toy villages. It was time to play and have some real Little fun with Marco.

And if Marco was anywhere near as good at playtime as he was with spanking, then Rex knew he was in for a wonderful time indeed.

Chapter 8

Marco

A few days later, and Marco was back in the MMA gym and building up one hell of a sweat. It was a cardio and endurance session, and Marco was pushing his forty-five-year-old body to its limits.

Marco could feel his blood pumping around his muscles, desperately trying to give him what he needed to keep on going. It was painful work, but the good kind of pain that meant progress was being made.

The gym was full of noise. A hardcore techno beat thumped and thudded over the noise of the trainers shouting out instructions and driving their pupils on toward levels they had never imagined possible.

Marco loved to be challenged in the gym. The feeling of being totally at the mercy of his trainer and with the sole goal of making a new gain or pushing his body even further was more than enough to motivate him.

The fact that the competitive fight with Aleksei wasn't too far off was only serving to add an extra level of determination to Marco's mindset as he grunted and thrusted his way through a brutal set of weighted thigh-thrusts.

'Okay, and that's a fucking wrap on that one,' Tyron said, smiling as he handed an exhausted Marco his water bottle. 'Fucking awesome work, Marco. You've got this.'

Marco nodded and attempted a smile. In that moment though, all Marco could do was sip on the water and wait for his heartrate to get back to something approaching normal.

The last few days of looking after Rex had been wonderful, and as Marco took in his rest period, his mind went straight back to Rex.

Rex may have been a little too over enthusiastic at times, but he was a good kid. Marco could see that Rex had absolutely everything it took to be the best boy a Daddy like him could ask for.

That being said, Marco also knew that as fun and fulfilling as it was to have Rex around, the primary concern was in how to best dispatch Kash Vialli and his men.

I have to do it right.

Kash is a punk, but he's dangerous.

He's growing his gang too, which spells trouble...

After putting the word out about Kash, Marco had learned that Kash was a man of ambition. He may have shown all the characteristics of a typical flash in the pan street thug, but sometimes they were the most dangerous to deal with.

This wouldn't be a simple case of putting a hit out and removing Kash from the scene. From what Marco could gather, Kash was attempting to place himself in the service of different gang factions across the city.

'He may be a flashy thug, but that's smart...' Marco grumbled under his still-heavy breathing.

Marco knew that you simply couldn't take someone out without permission once they were associated with a big boss. That kind of thing could be a complex, drawn out affair. If the rumors about Kash embedding himself in various gangs was true, then Marco would have to truly consider exactly how he was going to move.

Ultimately though, the goal was the same.

For Rex's sake, Kash was going down.

It was just a question of how...

But Marco couldn't dwell too much on Kash. After his rest time came to an end, it was straight back into another punishing workout. The only problem was that somehow Aleksei had worked his way over from the other side of the gym.

With his cocky smile and Russian gang tattoos fully on display on his sweaty, ripped body, Aleksei strode toward Marco like he was looking for trouble.

'Hey, Aleksei, take it easy,' Tyron said, stepping in between Aleksei and Marco. 'We don't need any shit going down. This is a fitness session. We ain't fighting yet.'

'Sure, whatever,' Aleksei laughed. 'I can see the old man is wasted. What's up, moving your body too hard in your old age?'

'*Plenty* enough left in the tank to smash you to pieces,' Marco said, growling as he stepped forward, not willing to give an inch to his cocky rival. 'Now why don't you just crawl back into your hole and let the big boys get on with things?'

Marco could see that he was getting to Aleksei.

But Aleksei had one round left to fire in his gun, and it was an explosive one too...

'Okay, old man,' Aleksei snarled. 'Oh, and by the way, your kinky secrets are safe with me. For now...'

Marco immediately felt furious. He wasn't sure whether Aleksei was referring to him being a Daddy, or even to his love of delicate panties. Either way, it was a low-blow and Marco had to focus extremely hard to ensure that he didn't give Aleksei what he so desperately wanted and lose his cool.

'Like I said, time for you to get back in your hole,' Marco grunted, standing tall and refusing to take a backward step as a grinning Aleksei cackled his way back to the other side of the gym.

What had been a thoroughly satisfying and intense workout had taken an unfortunate turn. Marco was angry. *Seriously* angry. It was time to finish off the session and get the hell out of there.

* * *

Marco arrived at the coffee spot and was glad to see a friendly face in Rocco. Taking a seat on the street-side dining area, Marco fist-bumped Rocco and couldn't help but get straight to unloading about Aleksei...

'This God damned asshole is too much,' Marco said, trying his best to remain calm but not exactly succeeding. 'I know what he's trying to do. Whether he knows about me being a Daddy, or my other kinks... I don't know, I just need to not let him inside my head.'

Rocco nodded and sipped on his double espresso.

'You're right,' Rocco said. 'But it's easier said than done. Trust me, I've been there myself. Assholes like Aleksei will always try and get any advantage they can, they don't know anything about respect or doing things the honorable way.'

'True,' Marco said, comforted by Rocco's support. 'The crazy thing is that I don't think he's bad all the way down. He's from a decent family, very respectable Russians with a long history of doing business the right way. I guess maybe he's just a bad apple.'

'Either that or he's got a thing for you?' Rocco chuckled. 'You know, this is how some guys go about showing their love.'

Marco and Rocco laughed together. This scenario was possible, albeit unlikely. Still, it was good for Marco to see the funny side to the situation rather than allow it to eat away at him.

'And if he does know something about your kinks, so what?' Rocco added. 'It might be a bit embarrassing, but you're

Marco Santino… not one single person will have the cojones to say anything. Not to your face, anyhow.'

'So what you're saying is that I definitely need to keep this beef in the gym?' Marco said, knowing full well what Rocco's response would be.

'One hundred percent yes, keep it in the gym,' Rocco said. 'You know the rules, man. What happens in the gym, stays in the gym. Unless you want a city-wide civil war breaking out? Jesus, that's the last thing we need.'

'I agree,' Marco laughed. 'You're right again Mr. Luca.'

'Damn right I'm right,' Rocco laughed, the pair of them raising their espresso glasses to one another.

The Mafia Daddies stuck together through thick and thin. It was important that they were able to talk and call each other out when necessary.

Finding truly loyal and open-hearted allies in the Mafia was a tricky business. The wrong word spoken to the wrong person could have deadly results, so having a close-knit group of diehard friends was something to cherish.

Speaking of which, Dante may not have been present for the coffee, but he sent a message to Marco and Rocco letting them know that they were in his thoughts…

Guys – make sure to have an extra coffee for me. I'm tied up with some pretty serious shit that's going down. I'm calling in a few familiar faces to help. I think when the time comes, we'll be good to make a big push and do something VERY big. Anyway, take it easy and see you soon. DANTE.

Marco and Rocco exchanged a knowing look. Dante was a seriously good operator, and if he said something big was going down, he wasn't likely to be exaggerating.

But with their coffees finished and a swirl of wind in the air, Marco and Rocco knew it was time to go their separate ways...

'My boy Eddie is due his weekly maintenance paddling,' Rocco grinned. 'I swear he's sassing me on purpose to make sure I give it to him good. Hell, I'm not complaining...'

'Ha! Well, I'm not at that stage with Rex yet, but it's going well so far,' Marco said, embracing his good friend Rocco before the pair of them turned and headed off in opposite directions. 'Take it easy, brother.'

'You too,' Rocco said, flashing a knowing smile and disappearing around the corner.

Suddenly, the drama with Aleksei couldn't have been further from Marco's mind. Now it was all about getting home as quickly as possible to Rex and seeing what his sweet little boy had been up to...

* * *

Marco opened the door to his apartment and immediately knew that something was amiss.

'Are... you... kidding... me?' Marco muttered, his quiet voice suddenly getting louder. 'Boy! Where are you? Come to me right this instant.'

As Marco waited for Rex to show his face, he surveyed the damage around him. Thankfully there was no damage to any of his furniture or works of art, but that seemed more like a tiny shred of comfort than anything to be overly pleased about.

The entire stretch of the main hallway was a total mess. There were trails of food crumbs, toys, even clothes scattered across the floor.

Marco needed answers, and he needed them quickly.

'Yes?' Rex said, biting his bottom lip and looking more than a little sheepish. 'I was going to tidy up...'

'Really? When? Tonight? Tomorrow? Next week?' Marco said, his voice firm but under control. 'That's not even the point. I'm all in favor of you having fun, but this is just out of control.'

'Jeeze, it's not *that* bad,' Rex said, kicking a toy car from under his feet. 'You should see the mess I make back at my place. If anything, you're lucky it wasn't worse!'

That was the last straw as far as Marco was concerned.

A verbal dressing down wasn't going to suffice. In fact, it wasn't even close to being enough. And neither would a hand spanking do either. It was time for the boy to feel the paddle on his messy, sassy butt.

'Come with me,' Marco barked, walking toward Rex and taking him firmly by the arm. 'It's time for you to learn that as a guest here, you need to show the basic respect of not turning my home into a total crash site.'

'Naaw*!* This isn't fair!' Rex squawked, stomping his foot on the floor. 'You're being a big, mean Daddy! I should be allowed to make a mess!'

Marco shook his head.

It was clear to see that Rex was being a brat, and it was time that he learned his lesson.

'You are going to show your Daddy that you know you deserve this paddling,' Marco said, letting go of Rex as they entered the bedroom. 'Pull your pants and briefs down yourself and present those buttocks for me. Do it, and do it now.'

'*Urgh.* Fine!' Rex said, stomping toward the center of the room and doing as Marco instructed. 'Happy?'

Marco looked at Rex as he stood in the center of the room, his naked lower half on display and his dick very much showing signs of excitement.

'Now walk over to the desk and place your hands on either side as you bend over,' Marco growled, his Daddy Dom instincts truly kicking in. 'If you thought your hand spanking was hard, you'd better be ready for a whole new world.'

Rex did as he was told yet again, except this time without and verbal sass. Clearly, the very real prospect of a painful paddling was becoming far more real to him.

'Good, but stick that little booty out a bit more,' Marco said, fetching his paddle from the cupboard in the closet.

Marco swished the paddle through the air and saw Rex's body tense up at the sound of it. For all of his bravado, Rex was clearly nervous now that the paddling was imminent.

'I will paddle your butt twenty times,' Marco said, his voice cold and in control. 'Your feet will not move from that spot. Not once. If they do, we start again from zero. Understood?'

'Y-y-y-yes, Daddy,' Rex said, his voice wavering. 'I understand.'

'Now, I'll have a few more warm-up swings and we'll be good to go,' Marco said, taking a moment to get his perfect swing motion in full flow.

Marco wanted this paddling to make a statement, and it was important to him as a Daddy that he gave the best possible account of himself. Marco wanted Rex to like him, but he was more concerned in this moment with ensuring that Rex learned that Marco needed to be respected above all else.

After prolonging the moment for long enough, Marco duly set to work on giving Rex his punishment.

The first paddle swooshed down and crashed onto Rex's cheeks, immediately turning them a glowing red.

'Good, you took that well,' Marco said, impressed that Rex wasn't up and hopping around and grabbing his cheeks. 'But we've got another nineteen to go. Let's see how we get on, shall we?'

'*Awww*, yes Daddy,' Rex whimpered, clearly anticipating what was ahead.

And as Marco continued to bring down his paddle and crack it onto Rex's little butt, Marco continued to be impressed by

Rex's resilience. In fact, Rex was taking the paddling so well that Marco wanted to make sure that Rex wasn't simply putting a brave face on things.

'Remember, boy, you can always use your safeword,' Marco said, pausing the paddling with ten left to go. 'There's no shame in it. I won't think any less of you.'

'No, I'm good, Daddy,' Rex said, evidently in pain but managing to hold it together. 'Paddle me. Don't hold back.'

'Don't worry, I won't,' Marco said, a hint of a smile on his face as he felt proud of his boy. 'Let's get this final ten wrapped up nice and quickly.'

With that, Marco unleashed two sets of five rapid-fire paddle swats onto Rex. Rex was gasping and whimpering in pain from the stinging sensation but was as determined as ever to remain in position.

'And... there's... twenty!' Marco bellowed, the final swat crashing down and echoing around the bedroom.

Rex remained in position, his submissive obedience impressing Marco a great deal. But Rex had taken his punishment, and now the focus was all on the aftercare as far as Marco was concerned.

Without wasting a second, Marco picked Rex up and cradled him in his arms before walking into the adjoining bathroom and breaking out his cooling creams.

'Daddy, that feels so good,' Rex said, his demeanor surprisingly upbeat. 'I think I realized something too.'

'What's that, boy?' Marco replied tenderly as he lightly massaged the cooling cream deeper into Rex's glowing butt cheeks.

'I *totally* deserved that,' Rex continued. 'I'm not trying to make excuses, but I think what made me act so wild was feeling so safe and secure again. You know, after everything that's been going on. I haven't felt like letting loose like that was an option since *that thing* happened with *you know who*.'

'That's a fair assessment,' Marco said, proud that Rex was showing good self-awareness while still owning his actions. 'But don't worry, soon enough all will be resolved and you can go back to living your life as you were beforehand.'

'Except…'

'Yes?' Marco said, lightly stroking Rex's smooth, blonde hair. 'Except what?'

'Except you'll still be a part of my life, won't you?' Rex said, hope in his voice as he looked up into Marco's eyes.

'Of course,' Marco replied. 'I think I'll be in your life for a very long time. As long as you want me there.'

Rex simply smiled.

Marco felt like a real Daddy for perhaps the first time in his life. Having Rex in the apartment was like nothing Marco had experienced. This wasn't a quick hook-up or infatuation. This felt like something else entirely.

Marco didn't want to tempt fate, but he couldn't help wonder whether the relationship between him and Rex was about to go to a whole new level, and soon…

Chapter 9

Rex

The *Peachy Playpen* may have been out of bounds for Rex at that moment, but he was determined to have some fun in his life again.

Being under Marco's care was so far helping Rex feel more confident and with this in mind he had arranged to meet up with his friends at a small, very discreet new Little club a short Uber ride away.

As Rex sat in the back of the Uber, he thought back to how well things had been going since he moved in with Marco.

Sure, it wasn't always easy to stay on Marco's good side. After all, Marco was older and had gotten so used to living by himself that he very much had his own way of doing things.

But on the other hand, the more time that Rex was spending at Marco's place, the more that the two of them were finding one another's wavelengths. Rex was certainly learning to be more careful around Marco's delicate and ornate furnishings, and Rex was cleaning up after himself far more too.

Rex also could see that Marco was loosening up just a little bit too. It was still very much the case that Marco liked things neat and tidy, but Rex felt good to see that Marco was making allowances for his slightly less fastidious approach to tidying.

It was too early to say precisely where his relationship with Marco was headed, but Rex certainly couldn't deny that he *wanted* it to go further. Rex had felt a surge of attraction toward Marco from the very second he saw him – even in traumatic circumstances, it was undeniable to Rex that he had a hot streak for Marco.

And of course, having pleasured himself in the shower to thoughts of Marco in his tightest, finest sportswear, Rex would have been a fool to himself to try and deny that there was a spark there.

Rex sensed that Marco felt the same way, if only for the very obvious sign of Marco's seemingly very chunky dick hardening in his pants every time he tossed Rex over his lap for a spanking.

But Rex didn't want to get too ahead of himself.

And anyway, this morning was all about having fun with his friends.

'Yup, just here thank you,' Rex said, a cheery lilt in his voice as the Uber driver pulled over and parked the car outside of the club. 'Thank you so much. Have a great day!'

The Uber driver smiled warmly at Rex and as Rex got out of the car, he simply couldn't wait to get inside and meet his friends. Mac and Eddie had messaged to say that they were already inside, so Rex knew he had no time to spare.

It was time to do what Littles did best.

It was time for some serious fun at the *Little Hut*!

* * *

The *Little Hut* was a wonderful space and all three friends were having a great time.

Rex was wearing one of the new diapers that Marco had bought him. The diapers were extra-absorbent and had dinosaurs wearing astronaut helmets all over them. To say that these were cute diapers would be possibly understatement of the year.

Mac and Eddie were wearing the sweetest diapers too. Mac was wearing a tropical beach themed pair with patterns made up of big, colorful beach balls and palm trees, whereas Eddie's diapers were all blue, green, and purple race cars zooming around a track made of clouds.

'*Weeee!*' Mac said, tracing his finger across the diaper and making believe that that cars were really racing from one side to the other. 'I wish we could all be in real race cars now!'

'Yes, race cars that could fly!' Eddie added, giggling as he rolled over onto his back and stared up at the ceiling with its warmly lit nighttime scene.

Rex felt so lucky to have friends like Mac and Eddie.

I don't know what I'd do without them.

We understand each other so well.

It's just the perfect bond...

Rex could feel himself relaxing in a way that he hadn't for some time. Kash Vialli was a million miles away, so far in fact that it would probably take the fastest rocket ship a thousand years to get to him. Well, that's how it felt to Rex in that moment.

The three friends continued to play and giggle together, regressing in a most peaceful and wholesome way.

'This place is super-nice,' Rex said. 'I know we love the *Peachy Playpen*, but it's nice to have other spots to come to as well, isn't it?'

'Hooray for the *Little Hut*! Mac cheered.

'Double hooray!' Eddie added, gently humming to himself as he cuddled up to his stuffie, Stripes the tiger. 'We all love the *Little Hut*! Stuffies and Littles together!'

At this point, the three Littles each held their stuffies above their heads and began to sing a song, making the words up as they went along. Rex was giggling and laughing as the three of them had fun improvising the song as they went along.

With the juice boxes flowing and the good time rolling, Rex was having just the best time in his new favorite place. So much so in fact, that he barely noticed that his diaper was almost fit to burst.

Fortunately, the Little Hut's resident friendly nanny, Miss Julie, was on hand. Miss Julie was in her forties and had a strong motherly energy with her curvy body fitting snuggly inside her Little Hut uniform of a pink skirt and pale blue blouse.

Miss Julie's blue eyes twinkled and she smiled warmly as she cast her eyes over the Littles...

'I think you three boys are due a diaper change!' Miss Julie giggled. 'By the looks of it I've got three heavy diapers that need swapping out for some fresh ones. Come on, who's first?'

The three Littles giggled and each one threw their hands in the air to go first. Miss Julie smiled and picked out Rex.

As Rex lay on the changing mat, he felt safe and secure as Miss Julie removed his old diaper, cleaned and powdered around his private place, and fitted him with a brand-new diaper.

'These are wonderful diapers,' Miss Julie said.

'My Daddy got them for me,' Rex said, proud to have such a considerate Daddy as Marco. 'He made a good choice!'

'He certainly did,' Miss Julie said. 'Now off you go and have some fun. I think it's Eddie's turn for a fresh diaper now.'

With that, Rex went back to playing with Ozzy and his toys.

The *Little Hut* was a new experience, and it was great to meet such a friendly and caring nanny as Miss Julie.

Soon though, it would be time to head home and see what Marco was up to. Rex may have been feeling nice and relaxed, but he was beginning to feel like he wanted some fun and games with Marco sooner rather than later.

After all, Rex wanted to say thank you to Marco for buying him such wonderful diapers that even his new nanny was impressed with them!

I think I want to take things further.

In fact, I know I do.

I just hope Marco feels the same...

* * *

Rex arrived back home from the *Little Hut* and was feeling about as relaxed and happy as possible. It had been a brilliant experience, and whilst it wasn't quite the same as being at the *Peachy Playpen*, it had been so nice to try a new experience.

'Daddy? Oh Daddy where are you?' Rex called out as he walked toward the kitchen.

'In here,' Marco said, a gruffness in his voice that had Rex wondering what might have happened in his absence. 'I'm in the office.'

'Are you okay, Daddy?' Rex said, walking into Marco's office and seeing him pacing up and down, his mind looking like it was deep in thought. 'Nothing bad has happened, has it?'

'Something bad is always happening in my world,' Marco said, a wry smile on his face. 'Death and destruction is part of the game. All you hope and pray for is that it doesn't involve you on the receiving end.'

'That's a bit deep for me,' Rex said, unsure how to handle things.

'*Urgh*, sorry, boy,' Marco said turning to face Rex. 'It's just been one of those mornings where solving one problem just leads to another brand-new problem coming into focus. I'm okay though. You look like you've had a good time?'

'I had a great time, and Miss Julie was as wonderful and amazing as you said she'd be,' Rex said, blushing at the memory of having his diaper changed so gently and lovingly.

'I'd heard good things,' Marco said. 'I'm glad you had a great time. As I'm sure that Rocco and Dante are glad too for their boys.'

Rex smiled. But as much as he could see that Marco was trying to come over as relaxed, there was still clearly too many thoughts buzzing around in his Daddy's mind to allow him to actually chill out and enjoy being in the moment.

This calls for another approach.

I think I might just need to be a little bit naughty.

Or... kinky.

'Daddy?' Rex said, walking over toward Marco, who was now seated at his desk. 'Can I sit on your lap for a minute?'

'Sure, hop on,' Marco said, a slight smile on his face.

'I think I want to tell you about one of my big kinks,' Rex said, snuggling his butt down on Marco's lap. 'If you want me to?'

'Talk,' Marco said, smiling and with an immediate look of arousal in his eyes.

'It's... sportswear,' Rex said. 'I really, really, super-really like sportswear. You know, like the kind you wear for your MMA training...'

No sooner had Rex uttered the words, he could feel a sudden hard bulge probing up against his butt. Rex's words had clearly had the desired effect on Marco, and the more that Rex elaborated on them, the more aroused his Daddy became.

Rex even began to grind his butt down on Marco's crotch, the feeling of the big cock up against his cheeks making Rex gasp as he continued to go into detail about his love of all things shorts, leotard, and soft, stretchy material related.

'I think you might like me talking about my sportswear kink, Daddy,' Rex giggled. 'I think you might like it a *lot*.'

And judging by the look of lust in Marco's eyes and his grunt of approval, it wouldn't be long before the spark between them would prove too much to resist...

Chapter 10

Marco

All the talk of Rex's kink was getting Marco seriously aroused. And it was also making Marco think that it might be time for him to open up to Rex in a similar way.

Speaking about his inner desires wasn't something that perhaps came naturally to Marco. After all, his entire life was built around keeping secrets, privately planning bank heists, and any other of the countless Mafia secrets and plots that he had to protect.

However, being at home with Rex gave Marco a different kind of outlook. And it was one that he knew he needed to act upon.

'Boy, you know I've got my own kinks too,' Marco said, trying to hide the feint hint of nervousness he was feeling about opening up himself.

Marco had long held his lingerie kink close to his chest. It was hardly the kind of thing that a notorious bank robbing Mafia man was ever going to openly publicize. The crime world could be judgmental, and so much of it was built on traditional masculine values.

The thought of a mobster openly talking about his love of soft, silky panties was something that just didn't seem possible.

With that in mind, Marco was understandably nervous.

I can still back out.

I could just come up with some BS.

No, I need to do this...

Marco cleared his throat and looked at an expectant Rex. Marco could see that Rex truly wanted to hear what he had to say, and based on his experience with Rex so far, Marco was sure that he would listen with an open mind and an open heart too.

'It's okay, Daddy,' Rex said, perhaps sensing Marco's reluctance. 'You can tell me. I won't *ever* judge you. Especially not after everything you're doing for me.'

Rex's words were fantastic to hear.

Marco knew it might feel uncomfortable at first, but it was his time to speak and share his desires with Rex, just like Rex had done with him.

'I like... panties,' Marco said, his heart thumping in his chest. 'You know, feminine, intricate, soft. I like wearing them. I get off on it. I'd love to wear some... for you.'

Marco paused. He could see that Rex was eagerly taking each and every word in. But what Marco didn't know for sure was how Rex would respond. After all, there was no way that Rex was anticipating this kink. Was there?

'That sounds... awesome,' Rex said. 'We've even got similar kinks. I mean, I know sportswear and panties aren't *the same*, but it's a similar ballpark. I think I'd like to try your kink. And if you'd want to try and play with my kink too, that would be... incredible.'

Marco was blown away by how open and mature Rex was being about this. Clearly, while Rex might have been a Little, he was more than capable of having a serious and open discussion.

It wasn't that Marco ever doubted that Rex would respond like this, it was more that Marco had never experienced anything like this with another boy before.

Marco was an expert in judging people's characters and spotting the tiny behavioral tics that gave away their true thoughts. This was a Mafia thing, a skill that Marco had been trained in and developed over the years. And as far as Marco could tell, Rex's response to his panty revelation was totally genuine.

Marco felt a sudden wave of relief and joy wash over him.

For so long, Marco had kept his secret so close to his chest. It was almost like his panty kink had been the combination code for the world's most sophisticated safety vault.

But now that Marco was able to share, everything seemed so much lighter, and there was of course the possibility that he might even be able to start enjoying his kink in ways he had only previously ever fantasized about.

'Boy, lean in close,' Marco said, smiling as Rex leaned in so that their lips were barely a millimeter apart. 'I want to kiss you. I've wanted to kiss you ever since... well, the whole damn time I've known you. But I want you to feel sure that you want it too.'

'I am, Daddy,' Rex said, and the pair of them touched lips and began to kiss.

The feeling of Rex's soft, sweet lips touching down on his was incredible, and just as electric as Marco had imagined it would be.

As the kiss became more passionate, with their tongues intertwining and their hands beginning to roam over one another's bodies, it became perfectly clear that the physical connection was every bit as strong as the emotional one.

Marco reached around and squeezed Rex's soft, peachy butt cheeks through the material of his shorts. It was a different sensation to spanking them, but one that felt equally as nice.

Rex was perfectly built for all of Marco's desires. He was slender, athletic, and had a supple and surprisingly strong feel to him – and Marco's mind was running wild with the kinds of positions that they could put themselves in...

Marco's cock was as hard as it had ever been, and every inch of his body was reacting to Rex's passionate full-blooded kissing. Marco had hooked up with boys in the past, although far less so over recent times. But never had Marco felt such a strong and all-consuming connection as he did with Rex.

This was going to be very difficult to hit the pause button with.

The animalistic lust in Marco wanted to strip Rex butt naked right there and then in the office and make him his. And the fact that Marco suspected Rex wanted the exact same thing made it all the harder to show restraint and do what, deep down, Marco knew needed to be done.

Marco had never allowed himself to be vulnerable enough to let a boy inside his thoughts like he just had done with Rex. And now they were passionately making out, their breathing heavy and all signs pointing in one direction.

But...

It was time for Marco be responsible and bring the kissing and fondling to an end – for now, at least.

'Boy, believe me when I say I'd like to let this progress,' Marco said, his breathing heavy. 'But we need to do this right. I think far too much of you to act irresponsibly.'

'I was enjoying myself! You don't need to worry about me,' Rex pleaded, the tent at the front of his shorts providing clear evidence of his claims.

'I don't doubt that,' Marco replied. 'But I'm a Daddy. And I need to act like one. We need to agree upon a contract.'

'A contract?' Rex said. 'You mean like how Eddie and Mac have with their Daddies?'

'You got it,' Marco said, walking over to a cabinet in the corner of the office and opening it up. 'Just like *this*.'

Marco walked back to the desk and put the draft contract down on the table. He could see that Rex was eagerly scanning his eyes over it. This was a good sign. And it was also positive that Rex knew about a BDSM contract through his Little friends.

'Wow, there's some interesting kinks on here!' Rex said, giggling as he read through. 'I'm not too sure about some of them…'

'That's fine. And that's the whole point of this contract,' Marco said. 'We check the ones we like, and the ones we *might* like, and we can put a cross by the ones that really don't do it for us. Hopefully we'll have a nice cross-section of interests between us.'

'We will, I know we will!' Rex squealed, excitedly working his way through the various kinks and niches.

As the continued to work through the contract together, both Marco and Rex confirmed that this would be a monogamous situation, and as both had recent clean sexual health results, they wouldn't use protection.

It was a pleasure for Marco to be finally taking this step with someone who was a true boy, but also had the maturity and understanding to take on board a contract and all the other nuances that came with an agreement like this.

Rex is one of a kind.

We met in bad circumstances, but…

All I know is that I'm glad we get to be together now.

With the contract all signed and sealed, there was no longer any need to hold back on their impulses.

The only question was which kink they would explore first?

Chapter 11

Rex

The idea of a contract made total sense to Rex. He had heard his Little friends Mac and Eddie talking about theirs and would listen with great interest as they talked about how it was a safe and clear way to explore kinks, both ones that they had and their Daddies' kinks too.

Of course, prior to meeting Marco the idea of one day having a BDSM contract of his own was nothing more than a fantasy for Rex.

A contract was a fantasy that seemed about as distant as the furthest star in the galaxy. Until now...

'Daddy, I'm so glad we've done this,' Rex said. 'I don't think I've had such a good day as today since... you know... *before*.'

Rex watched Marco smile as he picked the contracts up and carefully filed them away in a safe place in his office.

'Here, we'll know where they are now,' Marco said. 'But there's no danger of us losing them either.'

Rex smiled and blushed at the thought of trying out all the new and exciting things on the contract. Rex fiddled with his strawberry earring and felt his entire body tingle with the possibilities of what him and Marco could do together.

Rex may not have had much experience with other men, but that wasn't to say that his imagination wasn't fully versed in dreaming up different scenarios and fantasies.

With his and Marco's make out session still fresh in his mind, and the stimulation of reading and signing the contract very much of the moment, Rex decided that he would see if Marco was up for having some fun right there and then...

'Daddy?' Rex said, trying his best to not sound *too* over-excited. 'Would you... maybe... want to try something *now*?'

'You mean...'

'Yup, something from the contract,' Rex said, unable to stifle a giggle as he felt his cheeks flushing crimson red. 'I was thinking... maybe you could put on one of your MMA shorts or wrestling leotards?'

Rex wasn't sure how Marco was going to react. After all, Marco was the Daddy, and it was his role to call the shots in the relationship. Or so Rex assumed...

'Wait there boy,' Marco said, a huge grin on his face. 'Oh, you'll need to strip too. Right down to your briefs.'

Rex gasped as the reality of what was about to happen hit him.

Is Daddy really going to...

I can't believe it...

Could he really, really, really be...

In what felt like less than thirty seconds, Marco was calling out to Rex.

'Boy, come into the bedroom,' Marco bellowed. 'Now! And you'd better not be wearing anything more than those little tighty-whiteys.'

Rex finished stripping off and raced into the bedroom. And Rex wasn't disappointed at the sight that met him either.

'OMG, Daddy,' Rex said, his hand over his mouth in total shock and awe. 'You look... just *wow*.'

Standing before Rex was an image that could have come straight from his hottest, naughtiest late night fantasies – the kind of fantasies that would always lead to Rex pleasuring himself to the most satisfying solo climaxes.

Marco was wearing nothing but his tight green wrestling leotard. It left nothing to the imagination, as Rex would have hoped for. The sight of Marco's thick, elephant-trunk sized dick running down one side was enough to make Rex nearly start drooling right there on the spot.

But it wasn't just Marco's dick-print that was worthy of Rex's admiring looks. Marco's physique was spectacular. He may have been an older man, but Marco's body looked like it had been honed from the finest marble. With shoulders and biceps that looked strong enough to push a boulder up a mountain, Rex could see why Marco was known for his fearsome one on one combat.

There was something else that caught Rex's eyes too.

On the exposed part of Marco's rippled, well-defined chest were three small, circular scars. Rex couldn't be sure what the scars were as a result of, but he instinctively had his suspicions.

'It's fine to look, boy,' Marco said, clearly noticing where Rex's eyes had been drawn. 'And it's okay to ask about them too. But maybe save your questions for later. Now it's time to... wrestle!'

With that a delighted Rex squealed as Marco charged over toward him and picked him up with ease.

'Daddy, Daddy, put me down!' Rex giggled with delight.

'Certainly,' Marco said, flipping Rex down onto the huge bed. 'After all, we need somewhere to wrestle safely.'

Marco proceeded to put Rex into a variety of holds, easily manipulating Rex's body with his superior strength and combat skills.

As far as Rex was concerned, this was the embodiment of his sportswear kink. The fact that he was being wrestled and dominated by a leotard wearing Dom who also happened to be his Daddy just made it all the hotter.

'Kiss me,' Marco said, pinning Rex down and thrusting his lycra-clad crotch into Rex's face. 'Show me who the boss really is.'

'Yes, sir,' Rex said, eagerly reaching up and planting not one, but several kisses up and down the outline of Marco's pulsing dick.

The sensation of being so close to Marco's dick was intoxicating for Rex. It was frustrating too. What Rex wanted was to feel the flesh of Marco's seemingly very large cock.

As it turned out, Rex wouldn't have to wait too long for that…

'Now do the same, but this time swallow it too,' Marco grunted, pulling the stretchy material of his leotard to one side and allowing his dick to stand proud, hard, and free. 'The defeated warrior must show his respects to the victor, after all.'

Rex knew that Marco had all the power.

But it wasn't exactly a bad forfeit for losing the wrestling.

As Rex stretched his tongue out and took his first taste of Marco's thick, long shaft, he felt Marco reaching down toward his cock too.

The two of them began to work in tandem. As Rex would suck and slurp on Marco's wide, bulbous dick head, Marco would spit on his hand and work Rex's equally hard cock, up and down, pushing Rex closer to the edge with each stroke.

'Don't cum before me,' Marco growled, playfully slapping Rex's dick from side to side as Rex continued to swallow and suck on Marco's manhood. 'I say when you have your release. Got it?'

Rex nodded and spluttered a 'yes' in response, but his main focus was on maintaining his rhythm. Rex could feel that Marco was beginning to thrust his hips and tense his body.

Neither one of them would be able to last much longer.

Rex knew it, and Marco knew it too.

As the pair of them climaxed together, Rex did his best to swallow as much of Marco's cum as he could without coming up for air. Rex was determined to show Marco that he had what it took to pleasure and please him in every way imaginable.

Marco too was keen to milk Rex dry, ensuring to keep on jerking and squeezing Rex's cock until every last drop had been drained.

With both of them spent, they collapsed onto the bed next to one another. After allowing a few moments to get his breath back, Rex reached across to Marco's hulking body and put his hand on the half-on, half-off lycra wrestling leotard.

'Daddy, thank you so much for doing this for me,' Rex said, his voice full of emotion, but a sense of total satisfaction coming through too. 'I've wanted that for so long, but I never thought I'd be able to live out my fantasy quite like *that*.'

'It was a pleasure, boy,' Marco said, smiling. 'Trust me, I enjoyed that. It might be your kink, but I think we can safely say that it's opened my eyes to a whole new world now. I might even have to get you some sportswear too. Just image the fun we could have if we were *both* wearing it.'

Rex nodded and giggled.

'That does sound super-duper awesome,' Rex said, his eyes suddenly heavy and a post-orgasm sleepiness hitting him hard.

As Rex drifted off to sleep, his mind was filled with good thoughts.

That was so good.

Hotter than the sun.

And we've only just gotten started...

* * *

Rex woke up from his post-steam fun to the smell of something delicious cooking in the kitchen.

'Daddy? Is that you making food?' Rex said, his brain still not fully woken up.

'Well, it's not Ozzy cooking, that's for sure!' Marco shouted back, a good-natured laugh following soon after. 'Come on, get up. You can watch a movie while I finish off cooking. I won't be long.'

Rex smiled and got out of bed. He quickly put on a pair of his favorite ruby-red thick pajamas and walked into the kitchen with Ozzy under his arm.

'Ozzy so *too* can cook!' Rex giggled.

'Sure, sure,' Marco said, rolling his eyes in mock impatience. 'Of *course* he can.'

'I'll find a movie for us but I won't start it,' Rex said. 'And I'll check with you if it's suitable too.'

'Good boy,' Marco replied, stirring a big pot of ravishingly red pasta sauce.

Rex went through to the living area and patiently flicked through the available movies as he patiently waited for Marco to finish up cooking.

'And here we go,' Marco said, walking in with two big and wholesome bowls of his specialty tomato pasta. 'So... what kind of movie are you thinking we should watch?'

'I'd like to try a gangster movie,' Rex said. 'But only if you think I'll be okay watching it.'

'Leave it to me,' Marco said. 'I know just the one. And don't worry, with me here you won't be scared. I've got your back. Not just for now, but for as long as you need me.'

Rex smiled sweetly and felt his heart fill with a million butterflies.

Rex knew that he would feel safe and secure watching a gangster movie with Marco – just like he felt safe any time he was with Marco.

The feelings for Marco were getting stronger by the second, and Rex couldn't help but wonder just how far things might go between them. It was all very new, but Rex's heart was telling him one thing and one thing only.

I think...

No, I hope....

No! I'm sure... Marco might just be my Forever Daddy.

Chapter 12

Marco

Roleplaying, wrestling, and simply having fun exploring their kinks and interests was so much fun. Marco hadn't experienced a prolonged period of enjoyment in his whole adult life up until this moment.

A couple of weeks flew by, and Marco was feeling on top of the world.

Of course, there was always Mafia business to be getting on with. Plans had to be made, secret meetings had to be attended, and there was *always* the underlying threat of a rival gang coming to the fore and starting a war over territory or a perceived disrespect.

However, none of the worst-case scenarios had come to pass, and Marco was simply enjoying what felt like being close to a normal life.

The one area that Marco and Rex hadn't explored yet was Marco's love of panties, but Marco figured there was no need to rush things. After all, this was his longest held kink and he still felt a little bit unsure about fully letting go and taking the leap to explore it with someone else.

But it wasn't only the panties that hadn't been experienced for real yet.

Marco and Rex had made out and given and received countless blowjobs and pleasurable massages *all over* their bodies. However they hadn't gone all the way. Having sex was a big deal to Marco, and although he suspected that Rex was ready, for Marco it was too big a step to simply take without careful consideration.

Marco wanted nothing more than to take the final step and truly make Rex his boy, but he was determined to resist the temptation as long as was humanly possible. *The best things come to those who wait*, as the old saying went.

If there was even the slightest chance that Rex wasn't ready, then Marco wasn't going to push for anything to happen. Marco was beginning to feel very deep feelings for Rex, the kind of emotions that he hadn't felt for a boy before.

However, the time for thinking about Rex was over.

Marco was at the MMA gym and getting himself ready to stretch out before his session. With the music pumping and the atmosphere as hyped and testosterone fueled as ever, Marco was anticipating another grueling but deeply satisfying session.

And even better, Aleksei wasn't there...

'Any word on where he is?' Marco said, not wanting to show that he cared, but at the same time feeling like he wanted to know. 'Probably hungover from too much partying, right?'

'Nah, not this time,' Arden, Marco's stretching partner said. 'The grapevine is saying that he's been arrested and is trying to get bail.'

'*Hmmmm.* The so-called grapevine often gets it wrong,' Marco said, careful not to believe any rumor he heard without challenging it.

'No, this is legit,' Arden replied. 'There's a video of him being taken by the cops from outside some club over on the Upper West Side. This shit is one hundred percent real.'

Marco nodded.

As much as he disliked Aleksei, Marco always felt a bit reticent to celebrate another gangster being arrested. Gang warfare was one thing, and it was always a reason to celebrate when winning a war. But seeing the cops bring down a man wasn't the same. In fact, it was often the worst feeling.

Marco had known plenty of friends and foes over the years who had been sentenced to long sentences, some of them so long that release was pretty much an impossibility. It was no way for a gangster to go out. But everyone knew the risks, it was just another part of the life they had all chosen.

'Hey, we ready or what?' the trainer said, walking over toward Marco and Arden. 'We've got a big workout planned for today. And we'll be working on our choke holds and submissions too, so get your minds focused and let's get to work.'

The training session certainly was everything that the trainer promised, and more on top of that too. Marco was happy with his performance, and was looking back on it with pride as he sat in the gym's sauna.

I've got this fight with Aleksei.

I know I can beat him.

That's if he's out of jail in time...

Marco shook his head and took a sip of water from his metal drinking bottle. As Marco relaxed in the heat, he practiced his slow breathing techniques and let the air flow in and then out of his nose. It was tough to get the initial rhythm, but once he nailed it, Marco began to feel supremely relaxed.

However, as was often the case, Marco's thoughts ultimately returned to business. More specifically, Marco began to consider more about how he was going to take Kash Vialli down.

Kash is on the rise.

He's associating with our rivals.

I could kill two birds with one bullet...

The more Marco considered it, the more he realized that by acting swiftly and taking Kash out, he could benefit his Mafia family in a wider sense.

It was never good to allow your enemies to build up new alliances, and Marco knew that if he could eliminate Kash now, he would prevent such an alliance getting off the ground before it could do any damage to his own interests.

With his body dripping with sweat, and his aching muscles in need of a post-workout massage, Marco decided that it was time to put all thoughts of Kash out of his mind and focus on his physical recovery.

After all, Marco had an excited boy waiting for him at home and who knew what fun and games the rest of the day would bring...

* * *

Marco had taken a cab over to the MMA gym as his SUV was in the auto shop getting a new hidden compartment fitted underneath the rear seats.

It actually made a pleasurable change to be driven to and from the gym, and it was certainly nice to be able to sit and relax after what had been a typically beastly session.

As the driver negotiated his way through the NYC traffic, Marco was busy messaging his buddies, Dante and Rocco...

Did you hear that Aleksei Ivanov has been arrested? Word is that he's struggling to make bail. I'm crossing my fingers he does, because I'm feeling ready to give him a whooping come fight night. MARCO.

Did I hear about it? I was only a block away when it happened. Me and the boy were enjoying a spanking themed party over at Night Vision and it was all anyone was talking about. Could be serious shit for Aleksei... ROCCO.

Marco raised his eyebrows at Rocco's message. If other people had heard about Aleksei, then it really might be something serious. It wasn't long before Dante threw his weight into the conversation either.

Shit, you and your boy are always out on the town, Rocco. But, yeah, I heard about it too. I think it's some kind of assault charge. But what I'm hearing tells me that Aleksei should be out soon enough. You know his family has the dollars to pay his bail, it's just a question of whether they've lost faith in him and might refuse to pay out of principle to teach him a lesson. DANTE.

Marco scratched his stubble and ran his hand through his hair. As much of a pain in the ass as Aleksei was, it was never good to see a gangster living too fast and getting arrested for dumb things like brawling in a night club.

Still, ultimately Aleksei was not Marco's responsibility. Aleksei would have to take whatever punishment was coming his way, not only from the law but from his family too.

As the cab driver pulled up outside Marco's building, Marco made sure to tip him generously and wish him a good day. The business would have of course paid for Marco to have a driver, but Marco enjoyed living like a regular citizen from time to time. And even from a security point of view it was arguably safer to travel incognito in a run of the mill cab.

Marco bade a good day to the doorman and then made his way up to the apartment, eager to see Rex and find out what his boy had been doing.

However, the sight that met Marco's eyes was not what he was expecting. Although that wasn't to say it was a bad thing. Far from it, in fact...

'Boy... I... I don't know what to say,' Marco said, for once struggling to maintain his ice-cold composure.

Marco was standing at the doorway to his bedroom and almost had to do a double take at what was before him. With the window blinds down and the room's lighting set to a warm, yellowy glow, Rex was lying on the bed with a pot of lube and clear-glass butt plug next to him.

But more than that...

Rex was wearing a pair of pink, high-cut panties with a thong back.

'Daddy, I've got a pair for you too...' Rex said, reaching behind him and holding up a pair of black satin panties with a subtle frilly detail around the waistband that looked just about *perfect*.

If Marco had been in any doubt whatsoever that Rex was ready to take the next physical step in their relationship, then those doubts had right that second been consigned to the trash.

Rex was ready.

And judging by how hard his cock was, so was Marco.

He may just have been involved in a full-on training session, but Marco knew he had one more round of physicality left in him. And this was one match-up he was determined to dominate from start to finish...

Chapter 13

Rex

The wait for Marco to arrive home had been full of nerves, excitement, and the sheer thrill of the unknown for Rex.

The idea to welcome Marco home with a *big* surprise had come to Rex moments after Marco had left for the MMA gym.

Rex had been enjoying the fun that he and Marco had been having together over the last couple of weeks. Making a connection like he had with Marco was something that Rex knew didn't happen very often in life. Some people sadly never found their perfect match, so for Rex to sense it with Marco in every bone of his body was something special.

But Rex realized that Marco cared so much for him that he wasn't going to be the one who made the first move when it came to going all the way together. Marco may have been a thoroughly domineering and stern Daddy, but he also had a sensitive and deeply caring side too.

Rex appreciated that Marco wanted to take it slow, but at the same time Rex was frustrated. What Rex wanted more than anything was to feel Marco deep inside him. The mere thought of presenting his body for Marco's pleasure was enough to get Rex aroused, and the time felt right for it to happen.

After Marco had left the apartment to head for the gym, Rex waited a moment to make sure that Marco was really gone. Rex even checked in Marco's closet to ensure that he hadn't forgotten any of his equipment.

'Perfect!' Rex giggled, running into the bedroom and crouching down next to the bed and pulling out a small paper shopping bag.

Inside the bag were a pair of panties that Rex had secretly bought for himself so that he could surprise Marco when the moment felt right. And it certainly did feel like the right moment when Rex felt the soft, smooth material in his hands.

Rex had also purchased a pair of panties for Marco, and the idea of letting his Daddy explore a real kink of his was something that thrilled Rex and made him feel closer than ever to Marco.

But Marco wouldn't be back from the MMA gym for a couple of hours, so Rex decided to relax and enjoy a nice, ice-cold glass of water in the kitchen.

As Rex sat down with his tall glass, he saw a message pop up on his phone. It was Mac, and he wanted all the news...

Hey there. So... tell me what the latest with Daddy Marco is? Have you had to use your safeword yet? I know Mafia Daddies can be scary sometimes tee-hee! Mac XoXoXoXo

· · ·

No, no safeword yet! And things are going SUPER well too. I think today might be THE day... Rex XXXXXXX

Wait... you mean THE DAY... like THE BIG, HARD... SUPER-SEXY DAY? Mac XoXoXoXo

Yup, I think it could be. Gotta go, I need to make sure I'm all ready for when Daddy comes home. Byeeeeee Rex XXXXXXXXX

Wowzers! Good luck, and remember if you need to talk afterward, call me! Love, Mac XoXoXoXo

Rex put his phone away and smiled. It was good to have such a kind and caring friend in Mac. It was the same with Eddie too. Both Mac and Eddie had more experience with their Daddies than Rex did, and even though Rex was excited about what might be about to happen with Marco, he was still a bit nervous too.

The fact that both Eddie and Mac were only a phone call away made Rex feel a lot more relaxed. He knew that if he ever needed to speak to someone that wasn't Marco, he would have his friends ready and waiting.

'Okay, time for me to hit the shower an freshen up,' Rex said, taking a deep breath. 'I want to be just perfect when Daddy comes home. I want this to be the best moment ever... for *both* of us.'

With that, Rex happily skipped through toward the bathroom.

Rex didn't know exactly when Marco would be back from the gym, but whenever it was, Rex wanted to make sure that everything was just right.

* * *

To say that Marco had looked surprised on his arrival back from the MMA gym would have been an understatement. But once over the initial shock, it was clear that Marco was incredibly happy to not only see Rex in panties, but have his own new pair to try on too...

'These feel so good,' Marco said, pulling the black satin panties up his strong, muscular thighs and over his semi-hard cock. 'And you look incredible too, boy.'

'Thank you, Daddy,' Rex said, flipping onto his front and showing off the thong-back of his panties. 'What does my butt make you want to do?'

Rex began to bump and grind his crotch into the mattress, taking car to wind his butt up and down slowly and seductively.

And judging by the size of the bulge at the front of Marco's panties, it was clear that Rex was very much pleasing his big, strong, panty-wearing Daddy.

'Come onto the bed, Daddy,' Rex said, arching his back and pushing his butt as high as he could into the air. 'Show me how into me you are.'

'*Grrrrr*,' Marco said, unable to control his growl as he pounced onto the bed. 'I don't know whether I want to eat that ass or fuck it.'

Rex giggled and turned on his side and pushed his butt out in the direction of Marco's crotch. The pair of them began to rub up against one another, the feeling of their panty-covered dicks proving a hugely sensual turn on for both of them.

Panties may have been Marco's kink, but Rex was now appreciating exactly how hot a pair of slender, slinky panties could be.

'The material feels so good,' Rex whispered, his own dick straining and pulsing as Marco reached around and slowly ran his finger up and down Rex's silk covered shaft. 'And so does *that* too.'

Rex could feel Marco's hot, heavy breath on his shoulder.

It was clear that things were going to heat up, and heat up pretty soon.

'Don't worry Daddy, I thought this might happen,' Rex said. 'I cleaned up down there in the shower before you came.'

'Are you sure you want to do this?' Marco said, his hands running over Rex's small, pink nipples. 'You know I don't mind waiting.'

'No, I want this,' Rex said, almost panting. 'I want this *now*.'

That was enough conformation for Marco, who wasted no time in gently lowering Rex's panties all the way down onto his ankles and then off altogether.

'Now it's my turn,' Marco said, kneeling on the bed. 'Except, you can have the honor of pulling my panties down.'

Rex eagerly leapt up and pulled Marco's panties down, the sight of his huge, angry cock springing up making Rex gasp.

'I think wearing my gift might have got you even harder?' Rex giggled, grabbing his own erect cock, and squeezing on it.

The two of them then fell into a passionate embrace and began rolling around on the bed together, their hands and legs intertwining as they kissed and explored one another's bodies.

'Put the butt plug in me,' Marco growled, turning on all fours and presenting his ass for Rex. 'Lube me, then squeeze it in. Do it, boy.'

Rex gasped in a delighted shock as he followed his Daddy's orders to the letter. The sight of the plug easing into Marco's lubricated ass hole was spectacular, but if Rex thought that Marco was planning on taking a surprise submissive role, Rex couldn't have been more wrong.

Marco quickly re-took control. He was a Daddy Dom after all.

'On your back, legs up,' Marco said, his voice full of lust, and an animalistic edge to him.

Rex did as he was commanded and soon enough he felt Marco working plenty of lube in and over his asshole, making Rex whimper with delight.

Marco hooked both of Rex's legs up on his shoulders and got himself into position.

'I love you, boy,' Marco growled. 'And now it's time to make you mine once and for all.'

The sensation of Marco pushing his thick cock deep inside Rex's tight, wet ass hole was uncomfortable at first. But it was a good kind of discomfort, if such a thing existed.

And it wasn't long before Rex had taken Marco's full length inside him.

Marco began to work up his rhythm as he moved his manhood up and down, using his strength to hold Rex perfectly in place.

Each stroke of Marco's cock ended up with Rex's g-spot being massaged, and soon enough Rex felt himself shoot his load all over his stomach.

'Oh no, I'm sorry, Daddy,' Rex said, in between moaning as Marco continued to fuck him. 'I came before you.'

'It's all good, don't worry,' Marco smiled, gripping Rex's thighs and increasing the power of his thrusts. 'I'm... not... too... far....'

Rex could feel Marco tensing his grip and then there was the new but unmistakable feeling of Marco cumming deep inside him. The sound of Marco's heavy, deep groans of ecstasy was almost enough to make Rex hard again.

But such was the physical and emotional exercitation from both, the only thing they wanted to do was to collapse on the bed next to one another and lie calmly side by side.

'That was...'

'Yep. It sure was,' Marco replied.

'Did you enjoy it as much as me?' Rex said, smiling, feeling better than he had ever known before.

'Sure did, boy,' Marco replied, laughing. 'Now, quiet. We can talk later. Let's just enjoy the moment.'

Rex nodded and smiled as he snuggled up to Marco.

At the bottom of the bed were two pairs of panties. Rex and Marco may not have been wearing them for long, but Rex was so glad that he had included them in his plans. To have experienced his first time with Marco while also giving Marco the joy of enjoying his big kink was something that Rex would remember *forever*.

* * *

Mini's Bistro was its usual upbeat and busy self. Fortunately for Rex, he was with Marco and getting a perfect outdoor seat and table wasn't a problem at all.

'So, boy,' Marco said, sipping on his single malt whiskey. 'You feeling good?'

'I am!' Rex said, blushing at the thought of what he and Marco had been doing only an hour earlier. 'I'm so happy that you enjoyed my little surprise too. I was worried you might think it was wrong for a Little to do something like that.'

Marco shook his head.

'I *loved* that you did that,' Marco said. 'It's not easy being a Daddy sometimes. And when you're part of my line of business too? Hell, you don't know the half of it. Having such a kind and considerate boy like you makes life easier. Well, it does when you're not leaving a mess everywhere!'

Marco let out a wholesome belly laugh, and Rex couldn't help but giggle along too. Rex cast his mind back and recalled coming to *Mini's Bistro* for the first time with Marco, having only just unpacked his stuff on his first night at Marco's penthouse.

A lot had changed since that first night, that was for sure.

As the drinks and food continued to arrive at their table, Rex and Marco opened up about their past lives. It felt good to talk so intimately and in a way where both felt secure in revealing details that they had never shared with anyone else, not even their closest friends.

Rex even went into the deepest feelings that he felt about losing his father all those years ago. So much had happened to Rex since then, but Rex was happy to have found a man in Marco who he could share his innermost hopes, thoughts and fears with.

As the sun set at the end of a perfect day, something dawned on Rex. He had never felt so truly seen as he did when he was with Marco. Whether it was sexually, emotionally, or just all round appreciated – Marco was the Daddy of Rex's dreams.

I want Marco to be my Forever Daddy.

I think he might feel the same about me.

Just wait until the other Littles here about this!

Chapter 14

Marco

The sound of Rex sweetly reading out loud to himself was about as wholesome and positive at Marco could handle. Marco wanted to run over and give Rex a big hug, but decided to hang back and allow Rex to finish off the chapter he was reading.

The apartment was cozy and warm, the evening having been a quiet and chill one up until that point. The pair of them had enjoyed a basic but truly delicious pasta salad, and after dinner Marco had gone for a therapeutic bath. Working out most days was fun, but it did leave Marco nursing several injuries and it felt like each training session at the MMA gym would see him returning with at least two new bruises.

Marco was out of the bath and nearly dry. Padding around his bedroom, Marco took a moment to quickly check his emails and then cast his eye over that evening's sports fixtures.

It was a wonderful sensation to know that Rex was in the other room, reading and generally giving off the happiest vibe.

When Marco was fully dry, he walked over toward his closet.

Then, taking a moment as a thought entered his head, Marco paused.

I could always... surprise the boy.

He might... enjoy that.

I could even...

With a devilishly handsome grin on his face, Marco found his special drawer in the closet and breathlessly selected a pair of panties. These were pure white, with a thong back, and cut high around his hips.

Such was Marco's excitement that he was barely able to get the panties on in time before his cock went fully erect. Marco just about managed it though, and now it was time to surprise Rex.

Marco crept out of the bedroom and then down the corridor toward the living area. If Rex heard Marco, he certainly wasn't showing any signs of having done so.

Marco got closer.

And closer.

And closer...

'Surprise!' Marco said, placing his hands over Rex's eyes. 'Got you!'

'Daddy!' Rex squealed, putting his Kindle down and wriggling around in his bright red pajama bottoms. 'What's going on?'

Marco revealed himself in full, and it was clear from the look on Rex's face that he was very much in the mood for some fun himself.

'They look… *hot*,' Rex giggled, the immediate tent at the front of his pajamas making his feelings more than clear. 'They're so small too. They're making me feel overdressed…'

'I agree, boy,' Marco said, leaning over Rex and pulling his pajama bottoms right off. 'Allow me to help you with this…'

Marco got down onto his knees as a naked Rex lay on the couch, his pale, slender body fully exposed to his Mafia Daddy.

Marco began by running his tongue up and down the full length of Rex's shaft as he used his hands to massage and gently pull on his balls.

Rex moaned in pleasure as Marco then began to grip and jerk his shaft while kissing and then swallowing his throbbing, purple dick head.

'That's it, you thrust those thighs up,' Marco growled, watching as Rex made his pleasure perfectly clear. 'It's time for me to give you the full service.'

Marco wasted no time and began to swallow Rex's cock, ensuring to work his tongue and swirl it around Rex's shaft as it went in and out of his mouth.

Rex began to moan and breathe harder, his toned chest rising and falling as he struggled to keep his composure. Marco could tell that Rex wasn't going to last much longer and he made a concerted effort to give Rex the most explosive orgasm.

As Marco felt Rex shoot his load deep into his mouth, Marco felt a sense of real satisfaction. And it was clear that Rex wanted to repay his Daddy too…

'Your turn,' Rex said, breathlessly, his orgasm having taken a lot out of him. 'I want my Daddy to have what I've just had…'

Marco wasn't going to say no to this offer, and he climbed up onto the sofa and let out a long, relaxed breath as Rex gently climbed on top of him.

'Time for your panties to come down,' Rex said, his eyes wide and full of lust as he slowly pulled Marco's panties down and witnessed Marco's erect cock spring up from their silky safehouse. 'I'll leave them just here so you can still feel them while I get to work…'

Rex stopped short of pulling the panties all the way off, and Marco loved the sensation of being pleasured while his panties remained just at the top of his upper thighs.

Marco grinned as Rex began to squeeze and pulse his fist around his cock. As Marco shut his eyes and allowed Rex to do the rest, he felt nothing but the purest, deepest pleasure imaginable…

The rain battered against the window in Marco's office. It was late at night. Like, *seriously* late.

Rex was fast asleep in the bedroom, and Marco could even hear his little snores if he listened out carefully enough. After their fun and frolics earlier in the evening, the pair of them had watched a movie before going to bed.

But Marco hadn't been able to get to sleep.

The deeper Marco's feelings for Rex went, the more he knew that he had to work out exactly how to handle Kash Vialli. This wasn't a situation that had any wriggle-room for error. Any kind of mistake or misjudgment would put Rex's life in danger and that was simply *not* an option.

I must do this right.

It has to be a one-off strike.

I need to take one shot and make sure I don't miss...

Marco saw the security alert flash up on his phone. It was a message from the night concierge in the lobby. But this was good news. It meant that Rocco and Dante had arrived.

Moments later, Marco was answering the door to his two Daddy friends and the three of them were soon enough sitting on the comfortable bucket chairs in the corner of the office.

'Damn, this whiskey is *good*,' Dante said, his black polo neck sweater and tailored pants giving his classically handsome look a further boost.

'Hell yeah it is,' Rocco added, sipping on his whiskey and smiling. 'But we ain't here to talk about liquor, right?'

The three men looked at one another.

After a quick debrief between them, it became obvious that Kash Vialli's recent activities weren't those of a man whose ambitions were to make a quick name for himself and then burn out. It seemed like Kash had some serious ambitions, and this made him all the more dangerous.

'Kash has been making alliances and plays over on the other side of town, right?' Rocco said, a concerned look on his face. 'And that makes me think it's only a matter of time before he moves on *our* territory.'

'That'll be the *last* move he ever makes if that's true,' Dante said finishing his whiskey and pouring a new measure.

'We need to remove the problem before it gets any worse,' Marco said. 'I know I have a personal stake in this, but it makes sense for the business too. I need to remove Kash for Rex, and we need to sort this out for our own good too.'

'Are you sure this isn't too personal for you, Marco?' Dante said, a serious tone to his voice. 'When things get too personal, that's when mistakes happen.'

Marco could feel himself getting angry. He didn't like having his temperament questioned. He was a cold, ruthless gangster, this was his life. Yes, this was personal to him but there was no way he would allow it to cloud his thinking.

But Marco could see that Dante was merely doing what any good Mafia man, or friend for that matter, should do. Dante was simply applying rational thinking and covering all the bases. Marco ultimately had no problem with that.

'No, I'm good,' Marco replied. 'Trust me, I'm on top of this.'

'So we're agree?' Rocco said, interjecting. 'Kash Vialli is going down?'

'He's going down,' Dante said, raising his glass.

'He's going down and he's never getting up again,' Marco added, raising his glass too.

With agreement between the three men in place, there was time for one more drink. All three of them had sleeping boys waiting for them, but in this moment it was all about the bond between three Mafia Daddies.

Marco felt good to know that his friends had his back. Not everyone in the Mafia had such a close, trustworthy set of friends. Maybe it was the fact that they were all Daddies, or maybe it was simply that they were honorable men in a tough, deadly world. Whatever it was, the three of them worked well together and shared a bond that could never be broken, and certainly not by an ambitious street thug like Kash.

Kash Vialli might have been riding high and feeling like he was on the up.

But Marco, Dante and Rocco were about to show Kash that there are some lines you simply never cross – not if you want to come out alive on the other side, that is.

Chapter 15

Rex

Rex was wondering how to occupy his time. He was already down one box of fun cereal and had even had an extra juice box. There would be a spanking later if Marco noticed that Rex had gone over his allocated juice box amount, but as far as Rex was concerned it would be a price worth paying for that tropical pineapple and mango taste.

But Rex couldn't spend the entire morning eating and drinking. He wanted to go and do something. Before the situation with Kash, Rex had work to keep him occupied. Rex couldn't deny the fact that he missed the *Peachy Playpen* a lot.

My heart belongs at the Peachy-P.

It's always so much fun.

It doesn't even feel like work...

Rex let out a long sigh. He knew all of this was for his own good, and his protection too. But that didn't stop Rex from missing all the sights, sounds, and fun of the *Peachy Playpen*.

'What can I do Ozzy?' Rex said, picking his stuffie up and giving Ozzy a big squeeze. 'Maybe seeing as I'm eating so many snacks I should go to the gym? You think Mac and Eddie would want to come with me too?'

Rex made Ozzy nod his head in approval.

'Well that settles it, Ozzy!' Rex giggled. 'If you think it's a good idea, then it *must* be. I'll message Eddie and Mac now and see if they want to come.'

A couple of messages and a quick car journey later, and Rex was in the gym. The car journey over had been quick, and extra safe too seeing as Marco had put a Mafia soldier on security detail at the penthouse. The security was instructed to stay with Rex at all times and drive him wherever he wanted to go. It was a new experience for Rex, but he really did enjoy getting everywhere way quicker than having to walk or take the subway.

After changing into his pale blue shorts and crips white t-shirt, Rex was soon up and running on the treadmill where he was joined by Mac and Eddie.

Before long, the talk between the three friends turned to Marco...

'So... have you and your Daddy been *exploring*?' Mac giggled, briefly slowing his treadmill so he could sip from a large water bottle.

'I bet they have,' Eddie added. 'I remember when me and Rocco first signed our contract we were trying everything out!'

The three Littles laughed.

Rex couldn't help but blush. This was all still very new to him and while he was comfortable talking about most things with his Little friends, discussing kinks in public was perhaps a step too far for him at the moment.

'Maybe I'll say more another time,' Rex said, trying hard not to squirm too much. 'But we definitely are having a *fun* time, that's for sure.'

Eddie and Mac exchanged knowing looks together before the three of them burst into another round of giggles. It was actually difficult for Rex and his friends to stay running on the treadmills due to laughing so much, but they managed it somehow.

After completing their runs and then doing some core work and kettle bell swings, the three friends made their way into the locker room. After a quick shower to clean their bodies of sweat, they headed into the cozy little sauna.

It was time to talk *Daddies*...

'*Phew*, it's almost as hot in here as me and Dante got over the weekend,' Mac said, wiping his brow. 'It feels like the longer we're together, the more our bodies get into sync and the sex gets even more powerful.'

'Same,' Eddie said. 'It's like something so natural, and so... sexy... the way that Rocco just knows what I want and exactly how to give it to me.'

'Guys!' Rex said, giggling. 'What if someone walked in and heard us talking like this?'

The three friends giggled together mischievously.

The fact was that the sauna door was across from them and they would be able to cut short any X-rated conversation well before someone was able to hear what was being spoken about. Well, hopefully anyhow.

As the friends continued to talk uncensored, Rex began to appreciate just how lucky he was to be with Marco. Eddie and Mac had been with their Daddies for longer than him, but that enabled Rex to see into what it could be like if him and Marco became a true Forever couple.

It may have been a horrible situation that brought Rex together with Marco, but Rex was almost thankful that it had happened. Everything that Eddie and Mac were saying rang so true with Rex, and it made him even more determined to please his Daddy and have as much fun with him as was possible.

Marco may have been a notorious gangster, and Rex knew that there were sides of Marco's work that he would never want to hear about. But that wasn't the Marco that Rex called Daddy. It certainly wasn't the Marco who was open and honest about his own kinks and desires and who loved nothing more than sharing and being a loving, strict, and passionate Daddy to Rex.

'Guys,' Rex said, a nervous excitement in his voice. 'I think... want... hope... that Marco might be...'

'Say it! Say it!' both Mac and Eddie chanted, desperate for Rex to say out loud what they knew he was feeling.

'I think Marco might be my Forever Daddy!' Rex said, immediately covering his face and squealing with delight.

Just at that moment, an elderly and rather more uptight gentleman entered the sauna. The time for giggling and squealing may have been brought to an abrupt end, but as far as Rex was concerned, this had been the best gym and sauna he had experienced in a very, *very* long time indeed.

* * *

Rex arrived home from the gym just a couple of moments after Marco had returned from his own workout at the MMA gym.

'Daddy, you look all... hot and sweaty,' Rex giggled, his eyes immediately scanning over Marco's hulking body.

But why was Marco still in his MMA shorts?

'*Um*... did you run home from the gym or something?' Rex said, his eyes fixating on the tight, black shorts that clung onto Marco's perfectly muscular, round butt cheeks. 'I know you're tough, but isn't that a bit extreme?'

'Ha!' Marco bellowed, finishing off his post-workout protein shake. 'My trainer gave me a lift. I had a feeling you might be home around the same time as me and thought I'd treat you to the sight of your Daddy in his skimpiest sportswear...'

Rex blushed and giggled.

It was a treat to see Marco like this. There were a few bumps and bruises on his body, but that just made him look all the tougher and more rugged.

The idea of Marco having been strenuously rolling around and wrestling and sparring was enough to make Rex hard, but what Marco did next was just something else altogether...

'What are they Daddy?' Rex said, watching on as Marco took something out of his gym bag.

'What do they look like, boy?' Marco laughed. 'They're MMA shorts. Or they're *your* MMA shorts, I should say. I got them for you. Do you like them?'

Rex almost couldn't believe it. This felt too good to be true. His sportswear kink needs were being met so hard it was almost impossible to focus his mind and say thank you.

'I... love them!' Rex finally managed, taking the skimpy red shorts in his hand and stretching them out, the feel of the material in his hand making him feel excited and ready for some fun. 'Can... I try them on?'

'I'd be offended if you didn't,' Marco laughed. 'And once they're on you, why don't we have our own private wrestling session? I'll give you some hints and tips. You never know when you might need them, right?'

Rex immediately stripped down and got into the MMA shorts. They felt incredible, just like how Rex had always imagined. With the protective padding around the crotch area, they were super-snug, and the tight elastic material kept his butt cheeks perfectly poised too.

OMG this is wild.

Am I about to have a sportswear wrestle with my Daddy?

This is like a dream... except it's actually happening...

As soon as Rex was ready, Marco picked him up and carried Rex into the bedroom before slinging him down onto the bed.

It was time for one seriously strong Daddy to take his boy to wrestling school. As far as Rex was concerned, this was several fantasies rolled into one.

Rex was having the time of his life.

And judging by the look on Marco's face as he hooked Rex's arms above his head, the fun times were only just beginning...

Chapter 16

Marco

With the talk of Kash building his army of thugs and making connections across the city, Marco decided to ramp up his own personal security. He would have done this even if Rex hadn't been in the picture, but the fact that his boy was at risk too simply made Marco even more vigilant.

That being said, Marco was determined not to let a wild, unpleasant thug like Kash interfere in his life more than was warranted.

So, with the extra security of two Mafia soldiers maintaining watchful eye, Marco and Rex went out to dinner.

'After you, boy,' Marco said, holding the door open to the cozy little Italian place that was a secret to many, but an absolute must-go for all the true connoisseurs of Italian food in NYC. 'Age before beauty...'

'Daddy! Such a corny Daddy joke!' Rex said, rolling his eyes but unable to prevent himself from laughing.

'Hey, boys who don't laugh at their Daddy's jokes get spanked,' Marcus said, chuckling as they walked toward their table.

'I'd rather be spanked than laugh at your cornball jokes!' Rex said, putting on an exaggerated look of disgust.

'Well, we'll have to make sure we take care of that later,' Marco said, taking his seat alongside Rex in the snuggly corner booth.

The restaurant was compact, lit perfectly for a private, late-night meal in the city. The booth was comfortable, and the small, ornate candle a perfect extra touch.

'I love it here,' Rex said, looking around and taking in the sights.

'Same,' Marco said. 'I actually came here with my parents. So, yeah... many *many* years ago. Probably before you were even born.'

'You don't speak about them much,' Rex said. 'Your parents, I mean. I know it's a silly question, but do you miss them?'

Marco paused before answering.

He wasn't used to answering questions like this. As much as Marco and his Daddy friends had deep discussions, the topic of Marco's childhood trauma wasn't something that they'd ever got into. Or, more precisely, it was an area that Marco had actively avoided speaking about.

'*Um...*' Marco said, momentarily unsure how to respond to his boy's question.

'It's okay, we don't have to talk about it,' Rex said. 'Maybe I shouldn't have asked.'

'No, no, not at all,' Marco replied, wanting to make sure that Rex didn't feel bad for his innocent question. 'I'm *glad* you asked. And the answer is... I don't know. It's not something I think about a lot. I guess with my life always having some kind of drama going on I push things like this right to the back where it's hard to give them any attention.'

'Well you can always talk to me about it,' Rex said, reaching over and placing his soft, delicate hand on top of Marco's much bigger hand with its long, diagonal scar running across the knuckles. 'I know it's not easy to lose a parent, I've been there. But losing both of them, and in the way that you did. *Gee.* That's something else.'

Marco could see that Rex meant what he said.

So many people shied away from talking about their past, especially in such an unforgiving and super-masculine scene like the gangster world was. But simply having a boy who he could trust and share with was a revelation.

'Some days I just try to *remember* them,' Marco said. 'I'll never forget the sight of them being shot. And maybe that part of my brain will never be fixed, the part that thirsts for revenge. But as long as I can remember the good times with them, then I figure that will always keep me human, right?'

Rex smiled sweetly.

Marco returned the smile and leant over to kiss Rex on his forehead.

This may have been a very deep way to begin a date night, but such was the comfort and ease between them, Marco and Rex were soon back to talking about all their usual fun topics.

Rex was excited to tell Marco about his plans for returning to work when Kash was vanquished. Rex was especially excited about perhaps organizing a joint event between the *Peachy Playpen* and the *Little Hut*.

'We could have a big co-party in the park! With balloons and picnic food and games too!' Rex enthused, his enthusiasm both heartwarming and impressive too.

'I like the sound of this,' Marco said, sipping on his vintage red wine. 'Although with that many Littles in one place the Daddies might need to come with earplugs.'

'Who says Daddies are invited?' Rex teased, taking a small sip of wine.

'*Grrrr*,' Marco replied. 'How could it ever be a real party without Daddies?'

The two of them burst into laughter. Rex decided that he wanted to quickly visit the bathroom before the food arrived and Marco decided this would be a good moment to check in on Rocco and Dante...

Guys. Two things. One: we may have a big party in the park soon, so tell your boys to expect an excited message from Rex. Two: I've sent a couple of guys to scope out Kash's daily routine. I think we need to strike, and soon. MARCO.

• • •

It wasn't long before both Rocco and Dante responded to Marco's message, and both of them were very keen on both of his points.

Party sounds good. Why don't we time it as a celebration for when we take that scum Kash out? The boys can play and we can sink some cold ones and toast another Mafia Daddies victory? ROCCO.

Sounds great. But let's not get ahead of ourselves. Kash may be street level, but I've heard that he's got some serious weapons stored somewhere. We need to be careful, as I'm sure you're taking into account, Marco. Have a good evening guys, I've got an appointment with a paddle and one very naughty boy any time now... ;) DANTE.

Marco grinned. It sounded like both of his friends were on board with his idea, and it was also good that Dante was showing some restraint too. Marco knew though that as long as he kept his cool and did all of his usual strategic planning, Kash would be dust before too long.

'Daddy, no cell phones at dinner!' Rex said as he returned from the bathroom. 'Maybe *I* should spank *you* later?'

'*Pffft*, yeah right,' Marco said, shaking his head in disbelief.

But just as the waiter walked over and began to put the piping hot pasta dishes down on their table, Marco caught a glimpse of an unwelcome face entering the restaurant.

'You have to be kidding me...' Marco muttered.

'Daddy, what's up?' Rex said, noting how unsettled Marco looked.

Before Marco had a chance to explain, Aleksei Ivanov and a posse of three other men were standing at Marco's table.

'*Awww*, how sweet,' Aleksei sneered, looking over toward Rex and back at Marco. 'Word gets around. I thought I'd pop by and say hi to the happy couple.'

'You finally made bail, huh?' Marco said. 'I guess your parents gave you one last chance, right?'

'Screw you,' Aleksei said, his tone of voice obnoxious. 'I've got more money than you've got pairs of panties.'

Marco felt a surge of anger flowing through him and he banged his fist down on the table. This was totally unacceptable. Aleksei may or may not have been referencing Marco's kink in a disparaging way, but whatever he was attempting to do, it wasn't coming from a good place.

'Easy, old man,' Aleksei said. 'Remember, what happens in the gym stays in the gym.'

'I don't know if you hadn't noticed, but we're not in the gym right now,' Marco said, standing up and going face to face with Aleksei. 'So if I were you, I'd back the hell up and get the fuck out of this restaurant right this second.'

'Whatever, man,' Aleksei said, clearly unsettled by Marco's anger. 'Come on guys, let's bounce. This place sucks anyway.'

As Aleksei and his men left, Marco took his seat and looked over at Rex.

'That was scary, Daddy,' Rex said, a slight tremble in his voice. 'He's not nice. But I think you could kick his butt if you wanted too.'

'That's the plan, kid,' Marco said. 'But in the gym, not on the streets or in a restaurant.'

The pair of them began to eat their food and soon enough Rex was happily chirping and describing in more details his plans for a big Little party in the park.

Marco nodded along as enthusiastically as he could as Rex spoke. But under the surface he was angry. Marco was angry at Aleksei for showing up with bad intentions. More than that though, Marco was furious at himself for falling into Aleksei's trap and showing so much emotion.

This didn't bode well for their fight.

And it also wasn't a good look for a respected Mafia man to be seen losing his cool in public either.

The sooner I kick this asshole's ass, the better.

Time to train harder. Push myself further.

Aleksei might not know it, but his MMA career is about to come to an end real soon...

* * *

The remainder of the meal passed without incident and Marco did a good enough job of hiding his unhappiness at what had gone down with Aleksei.

But there would be no fun and games on arrival back at the penthouse.

Rex was disappointed by this, but he understood Marco's need to put some hours in working on the bank heist. Marco's intention had been to drill down into some of the tiny, practical details of the job but the reality was that he spent most of his time brooding over Aleksei.

As Marco shut the office door and poured himself a whiskey, he walked over toward the large window that looked out onto the city below.

'So many people, just living their lives,' Marco said, his voice gravelly and full of richness. 'We've all got problems. But sometimes I wish for the simple life. The nine to five. Fuck, who am I kidding?'

Marco knew that as appealing as a simpler life might be, it just wasn't what he was cut out for. Marco's destiny had always been the Mafia. Having grown up in a household where his father was Mafia, and his father before him, there was never really any doubting as to what path Marco would choose.

'Mom, Dad, I miss you,' Marco said, raising his whiskey glass to the night sky outside the window. 'Here's to another year. And here's to Rex, I think you'd love him almost as much as I do.'

Marco turned away from the bustling night streets beneath and paced around the office. But try as he might, he couldn't keep the night of his parents murders out of his mind.

The sound of the gun, my mother's scream too.

My father collapsed in a heap on the floor.

No child should have to remember horrors like that.

Marco finally managed to pull himself out of a series of flashbacks from that fateful night. He knew he had to focus on Kash Vialli. Yes, Aleksei was a problem, but he couldn't be compared to Kash. It wasn't even close.

While Aleksei was a pain in the ass and a disrespectful sonofabitch, Kash was something else entirely. It was like Kash was evil to the core. Marco hadn't told Rex for risk of scaring him, but the more Marco had learned about Kash, the worse things got.

It turned out that Rex wasn't the only Little that Kash had terrorized or threatened. And with each new story or report that Marco heard about, his determination to wipe Kash out grew stronger.

'He needs to go, and I need to be the man to do it,' Marco said, taking a seat at his desk and turning his iMac on. 'I can't fuck this up. Rex is depending on me, and so are all the other boys in the city too.'

Marco knew that his fight with Aleksei could be resolved in the ring. But Kash was going to need to be fought in a world without rules, trainers, or the safety of a training gym.

It was time to take the gloves off and deliver a knockout blow...

Chapter 17

Rex

The sound of his morning alarm woke Rex in double-quick time. Each bleep rang like a foghorn in Rex's previously sleepy ears.

'Okay, okay!' Rex said, his half-closed eyes searching for the alarm so that he could put it out. 'Fine, I'll wake up!'

Rex sat up on the edge of the bed and could see that Marco was already up. Either that, or Marco hadn't come to bed at all. Rex knew that Marco had a lot going on in his life, and that sometimes he actually needed to stay up all night.

I hope Marco doesn't think my situation with Kash is too much.

I don't want to stress my Daddy.

I just want my fun life back...

Rex gave Ozzy a good morning kiss and cuddle and then stood up. Rex was wearing his red pajama bottoms and nothing else. Fortunately, Marco's penthouse had a top-of-the-line heating system, plus the bedroom had underfloor heating that felt all warm and toasty on Rex's feet.

'What shall I do today?' Rex wondered out loud. 'Daddy? Daddy? Where are you?'

'Working, boy,' Marco shouted, his voice coming from the kitchen. 'I've made you a smoothie too. Come on, come and get it.'

Rex hopped, skipped, and jumped his way out of the bedroom and down the corridor toward the large, airy kitchen.

Marco was sitting at the big kitchen table with two iPads and an A4 sketchpad too.

'Looks complicated,' Rex said, a smile on his face as he kissed his Daddy's cheek. 'Is this bank heist planning?'

'What gave it away?' Marco said, pointing at the diagram of the internal workings of a safe on his sketchpad. 'Come on, drink your smoothie. You need those morning vitamins.'

'Yes, Daddy,' Rex said, cheerily drinking the surprisingly tasty smoothie. 'You know when we were talking about your parents at the restaurant, and you said you never had much of a chance to talk about it?'

'*Uh-huh*, yeah?' Marco said, engrossed in his safe diagrams.

'Well I had an idea,' Rex continued.

'Go on,' Marco replied, now looking at Rex and giving Rex his full attention.

'A Little friend of mine called Sammy Tully has got a Daddy called Adonis,' Rex said, hope in his voice. 'Adonis is a therapist who helps people at The Little Club NYC and although he specializes in BDSM now, he is fully qualified in dealing with grief and things like that.'

Rex waited for a response from Marco. He could tell that Marco was thinking about what he said, but Rex couldn't work out if that was a good thing or a bad thing.

'It was just a suggestion,' Rex said.

'And I like it,' Marco replied. 'I'm too busy right now, you know that. But I think when I've cleared my schedule of one or two problems, that's something I'll investigate. Thank you, boy. I'm lucky to have you in my life. I really mean that.'

Rex smiled and began to drink his smoothie. It felt good to be of help to Marco, especially considering all the good things that Marco had done – and continued to do – for him.

'I think I'm going to go out to pick up some coloring pencils, Daddy,' Rex said. 'Once I'm done with the smoothie, I'll change and go. Just to the store at the corner. That's okay, right?'

'That's fine, one of my men will follow close behind,' Marco said, touching one iPad screen before shifting his attention to the other. 'And thanks again for recommending...'

'Adonis. Dr. Adonis Ranger,' Rex smiled. 'Are you getting forgetful in your old age?'

'*Grrrr*! I'll have none of that sass!' Marco laughed, before going back to studying his screens.

Rex could see that Marco was engrossed in his bank heist plans.

It was time to finish the smoothie, get changed, and go out to buy some wonderful new colors. A nice lazy day at the apartment sounded good, and what better way to spend it than coloring, drawing, and maybe even filling a diaper or two.

* * *

Rex took his first step out of the apartment building's entrance door and before he could even feel the rays of morning sun hit him, his face totally drained of all its color.

'No... no... it can't be....,' Rex said, freezing on the spot. 'That looks like... *him*.'

Rex felt paralyzed by fear.

Suddenly time seemed to stand still as a sickening feeling enveloped Rex's entire body.

Across on the other side of the road was a large, blacked-out SUV with a group of men standing around it, with nasty looks on their faces like they were full of bad intentions.

Amongst the men was... Kash.

Or it certainly looked like Kash as far as Rex could see.

In a state of panic, Rex turned to the security guard and said he was going back up to the apartment. Without waiting to give an explanation, Rex ran as fast as his legs would carry him all the way over toward the penthouse elevator.

'Come on, come on, come *on*!' Rex cried, his bottom lip trembling as he waited for the elevator to make its pinging noise.

It felt like an eternity, but a panicky Rex finally arrived at the penthouse level and immediately ran into the kitchen.

'Daddy? Where are you?' Rex hollered, desperately looking for Marco.

Marco ran out of the office and immediately made a beeline for his boy.

'What's wrong? What's happened?' Marco said. 'Calm yourself down and tell me, boy.'

'It's… h-h-h-him,' Rex stammered. 'Kash… I think I saw him outside.'

'You *think*?' Marco said. 'Was it him or not? This is important.'

'I… I… can't say for sure, I was so scared,' Rex said, struggling to maintain any kind of composure.

'Okay, one second,' Marco said.

Rex watched as Marco called his security detail. The look on Marco's face said it all. Marco suddenly shifted into a different mode. He may still have been Rex's Daddy Marco, but Marco was now also clearly a mobster with Mafia blood running through his veins.

'Boy, we're getting you out of here,' Marco said, a look of steely focus in his eyes. 'There's no time to talk. Just follow my instructions. You'll go with one of my security guys. He'll get you safe. Once you arrive, you *do not* move until I contact you. Got it?'

'But… I don't want to leave you,' Rex said, a tear falling down his cheek. 'I'm scared. I need to be with my Daddy.'

'And you will be,' Marco said, firmly. 'But not now. You need to let me handle my business. This is what I do, boy. You have to trust me.'

Rex nodded his head and struggled to hold back a waterfall's worth of tears. Rex's mind was ablaze with possibilities, and none of them were good.

What if Kash and his men killed Marco?

What would stop Kash from coming after him next?

The thought of being separated from Marco right now was bad enough, but what if this was the last time Rex ever saw his Daddy?

These thoughts were too difficult to bare. But fortunately for Rex, he didn't have any time ponder them. Before he knew what was going on, Marco was instructing his security to take Rex out of the basement carpark in one of their alternate, low-key cars that they used for covert work.

Rex wanted all of this to be over. And he wanted it to be over *fast*.

But Rex felt hopeless. All he could do was hope that his Daddy was going to handle Kash once and for all and then things could finally get back to normal.

* * *

Eddie's place was quiet and it felt good to be in friendly company. Eddies's Daddy Rocco had gone to be with Marco, and the two Littles were safely hidden away where no one could find them.

That being said, Rocco's trusted security guy was manning the property just in case. You could never be too safe, and Rocco made sure to tell his man to be extra vigilant before he left.

As Rex sat on the large, colorful couch, Eddie handed him a hot apple and cinnamon tea.

'Drink this, Rex,' Eddie said. 'You'll feel so much better.'

'Thank you,' Rex said, a sad look on his face. 'I don't know what to think. Or what to do. I feel so... *useless*.'

'Don't be sad,' Eddie said. 'Our Daddies are the best. And they'd do anything to keep us safe. I promise.'

Rex smiled.

Eddie could always be relied upon to be brave and optimistic too. But Rex knew that Eddie being optimistic wouldn't actually have any real effect on what might happen between Marco and Kash.

In that moment, Rex was finding his mind being torn between his fears for the future and flashbacks to the past. Losing his father when he was younger and then feeling so lost without him had really hurt Rex for so long. The thought of losing another important man in his life was almost too difficult to contemplate.

'Donut?' Eddie said, smiling as he picked up a big box of colorful donuts and passed it to Rex. 'You can have first choice.'

'Thank you,' Rex said, wiping a tear away. 'Thank you for being such a good friend to me.'

Rex ate the donut, but despite it being one of his favorite strawberry iced, double-cream donuts, it lacked any flavor whatsoever. Rex knew it was just him, but at the moment there was no way he could enjoy food.

In fact, Rex couldn't possibly have enjoyed anything at all right then.

Each and every car that passed down on the street below made Rex jump with fright. Every shouted voice from outside made him shudder.

'This might be a long night,' Eddie said, putting his arm around Rex and bringing him in close. 'Let me find a Disney movie and we can at least *try* to take our minds off things.'

Rex nodded, but he knew it wouldn't be that simple.

In that second, Rex didn't even care about getting revenge on Kash. All he wanted was his Daddy back safe and in one piece.

All Rex wanted was to know that Marco was safe...

Chapter 18

Marco

Whether or not Rex's sighting of Kash was genuine or not, the cold facts were that Kash didn't appear to be near Marco's building. There was simply no sight of him at all, and that was after several of Marco's security detail scanning the immediate area.

Perhaps it wasn't Kash who Rex had seen?

Or maybe Kash just happened to be in the area for another reason?

But Marco felt certain that if Kash had been there and with the intention of doing something serious it would be obvious by now.

What this scare had shown though was that the situation had come to a head. It simply couldn't go on any longer, that much was for sure.

It was with this in mind that Marco and Rocco headed to a nearby bar to gather their thoughts and see exactly what could be done in the here and now. But what Marco hadn't banked on was some troubling news from Rocco...

'Sorry, say that again?' Marco said, a look of disbelief on his face as he gripped his beer bottle so tightly it might have exploded.

Marco waited for Rocco to answer.

The bar was quiet, dimly lit, and had the old-style dive bar vibe that Marco enjoyed. An old classic jukebox played songs from the 1970s, and the small groups of drinkers nodded along as they sipped their drinks. But this wasn't a time for fun as far as Marco was concerned.

'Rocco?' Marco said, wanting his friend to repeat what he had just said, a rising impatience building in him.

'I'm sorry, man,' Rocco replied, genuine remorse in his voice. 'I spoke with the elder bosses, and they said we can't touch Kash. It's a political thing with the rival families. We can't lay a finger on Kash. If we do, it will risk a city-wide war that the top bosses simply don't want right now. We're screwed. There's no other way we can handle this.'

'Fuck,' Marco replied, briefly burying his head in his hands. 'But can't we say something to them, try to change their minds somehow?'

'I tried,' Rocco said. 'But the message coming back to me was very much along the *don't you fucking dare try and covert shit* lines. Anything happens to Kash, and the finger will be pointed at us. And if it's us or a full-blown war, we'll be the ones to get taken out. Both of us know that's true.'

Marco knew that Rocco was right.

It wasn't easy to hear this news, and it presented Marco with a real dilemma. Marco knew that Rex would never feel comfortable in the city again for as long as Kash was wandering the streets. The threat would always be there. And that was without mentioning all the other boys who Kash was no doubt terrorizing and making their lives a living hell.

'I don't know how I'll tell the boy,' Marco said, sipping on his beer. 'I just... fucking... can't believe this shit. Can you?'

Rocco sighed.

'Brother, the elder bosses will always think of the business first,' Rocco said. 'As high up as we are, or Dante for that matter, none of us are at the top, *top* level. We can call the shots day to day, but if the orders come from above, then we have no option but to follow them. Rebelling against the elder bosses is suicide, you know that.'

'You're right,' Marco said, frowning. 'And if we did make a move against their wishes, we'd be putting our boys in danger too. I just can't see a way around this. It's all messed the fuck up.'

'I think it's time for another drink, don't you?' Rocco said, signaling over toward the bartender.

Marco nodded, but his mind was elsewhere.

As far as Marco was concerned, the day was going from bad to worse. In some ways, it might have been better had Kash been outside the building for sure and making a play to storm in all guns blazing. At least that way Marco could have taken him out with the justification of self-defense.

But now that Marco had been told by Rocco about the situation involving Kash and the senior bosses, any kind of plausible deniability was gone.

As much as it pained him to think about it in these terms, perhaps his window of opportunity to take Kash out had gone. And maybe even gone for good?

With a pensive, deeply unhappy look on his face, Marco picked his bottle up and took the final sip of crisp, cold beer into his mouth. This situation wasn't going anywhere, and now Marco knew that he had to tell Rex.

How am I going to tell the boy?

The one thing I promised I'd do... and now I can't do it.

What the hell will Rex think when I tell him?

* * *

The journey from the bar to Rocco and Eddie's house was tense. Both Marco and Rocco knew that this wasn't how they wanted the situation to play out.

It was always a delicate issue when it came to taking orders from the higher ups in the upper echelons of the Mafia world. Respect for the elders was considered one of the things that separated the Mafia from other kinds of mobster organizations. When the orders came from the top, you were expected to listen and follow. Failure to fall into line would often result in the harshest possible sanctions.

'I don't know if Rex is going to understand how hard this is,' Marco said, pausing at the door to Rocco's place.

'Well, there's only one way to find out,' Rocco replied, patting his good friend on the shoulder. 'Whatever happens, I've got your back, okay?'

'Thank you, brother,' Marco said, a steely determination to deliver the news to Rex in as clear and calm a way as possible coming over him.

As they entered the building, Marco took a deep breath. He knew that this was a big moment, and he wanted to minimize the upset that Rex would undoubtedly feel. But as much as he tried to feel positive about his prospects of succeeding, Marco felt less than optimistic about his chances of success.

'Daddy! Yay!' Rex said, charging over toward Marco as he entered the kitchen. 'Did you... you know... make stinky Kash go away *forever*?'

'Boy, we need to talk,' Marco said, a serious tone in his voice.

'Okay, Eddie, come with me,' Rocco said. 'These two need a moment alone to talk.'

'*Huh*? Is everything okay?' Eddie said, a worried look on his face.

'Boy, come with me right now,' Rocco barked. 'I'll explain it to you, but Rex and his Daddy need a moment to themselves.'

With that, Rocco and Eddie left the kitchen and retired to their bedroom. Marco looked over toward Rex and could see that the initial look of optimism on his boy's face had been replaced by something else altogether.

'It's not good news, is it?' Rex said, a quiver in his voice as he struggled to hold it together.

'No, it's not,' Marco replied, taking a step toward Rex but holding back from going any closer. 'I'm going to say this as clearly as I can. It's not what you want to hear, and it's not what I wanted to hear either.'

'I don't understand,' Rex said. 'I thought…'

'Very clear instructions have come down to me from my bosses,' Marco said, hating every word that was coming out of his mouth. 'We can't touch Kash. Not now, maybe not ever. I'm so sorry. But if I move on Kash, all of our lives will be in danger. You have to understand that.'

'Well I *don't* understand it!' Rex said, stomping his feet on the ground as tears began to form in his eyes. 'You promised! And when Daddies promise, they're meant to stick to it!'

'Yes, but this is complex-'

'I don't care!' Rex shouted, his cheeks red and tears running down them like waterfalls. 'You promised, you promised, you promised!'

'Enough, boy!' Marco barked. 'I tried everything. I was close to making the move. We had every intention of wiping Kash out. But when the orders came from above us, we had no other option but to back off. You need to understand that this is about more than just you.'

Marco immediately regretted his choice of words.

Nothing was worth more than Rex, certainly not as far as Marco saw it. But whichever way he put it, Marco needed Rex to understand that he simply didn't have a realistic choice to go after Kash now.

'*Urgh*! Whatever!' Rex said. 'It makes no difference what you say. You said you'd avenge me, and you didn't. Now how am I ever meant to have a normal life again with that horrible jerk walking around the city?'

Before Marco could say any more, Rex charged past him and ran into Eddie's bedroom and slammed the door firmly shut behind him.

'Boy, please!' Marco called out, slamming his fist down on the oak worksurface in sheer frustration.

Marco looked up and saw Rocco.

'What the hell just happened?' Marco said, shaking his head. 'I knew he wouldn't react well, but...'

'The boy needs time,' Rocco said. 'You did what you could tonight. Why not let him stay over here with us, then I'm sure when he's calmed down a bit you both can work this out. You've got this, brother. I know you'll find a way to make things work.'

'I hope so,' Marco said, resigned to the fact that Rocco was right. 'I really fucking hope so.'

With that, Marco turned and walked out of Rocco and Eddie's place.

Marco would be spending the night alone back at his place. His only hope was that this would be a one-off, and not something far more permanent.

Chapter 19

Rex

Two long, miserable days passed before Rex returned to Marco's apartment. It was a confusing time for Rex, that was for sure. He wasn't from the Mafia world, so it was difficult to fully comprehend how the hierarchies operated and just how deadly serious they were taken too.

Rex may not have understood why Marco couldn't go against the wishes of his bosses, but he truly didn't want to entirely give up on him and Marco.

However, try as he might, Rex couldn't shake the feeling of having been let down by his Daddy. Logically, Rex could see that Marco wouldn't have backed down from taking Kash out unless it was a serious reason, but emotionally Rex simply felt the way he felt.

All in all, the atmosphere at Marco's penthouse wasn't good.

In fact, it was pretty terrible...

'I'm bored,' Rex said, shutting the refrigerator door a little too forcefully. 'And there's no treats in here either.'

'Careful! You'll break the mechanism,' Marco replied, a strong suggestion of impatience in his voice. 'Maybe there would be treats if you hadn't finished them all earlier?'

'*Urgh*, whatever,' Rex said, his voice sullen and lacking in the usual spark.

Rex wandered out of the kitchen and began kicking around some of his beanbag toys. The toys slid across the varnished floor at quite a pace, but Rex took little joy from it.

Why can't Marco just go against his bosses.

Just once... for me.

He knows how much this means to me...

Rex looked over at Marco and watched as he stared at his iPad screen, seemingly in deep concentration. Rex didn't know what could possibly be so interesting that it would take all of Marco's attention away from him.

'If you'd rather me go out so you can concentrate, I will,' Rex said, hands in his pockets as he idly kicked another beanbag all the way down the corridor toward the penthouse entry door. 'I'm not bothered either way.'

Rex was trying to provoke a reaction from Marco.

So far, Marco was remaining focused on his work, whatever that was.

At this point, Rex was running out of options. He wanted to elicit some kind of response from Marco, so decided to push a little harder...

'*Wheeee!*' Rex cried, flicking up a beanbag with his foot and kicking it across the kitchen, only narrowly missing Marco's head.

'What the hell?' Marco barked, his deep baritone voice echoing around the high ceilings. 'You're obviously still pissed off with me. But don't you think that I'm frustrated and angry about the situation too? I know it was you who suffered under Kash, but I took your pain on as my responsibility. And now I'm being prevented from helping. That hurts me *deeply*, boy.'

'Argh, this again!' Rex snapped back. 'You say you can't help. But why can't you, just once, go against what your bosses say? And don't tell me that I won't understand because it's a Mafia thing. Why can't this be a Daddy and Little thing instead? Just for once put something else ahead of the silly, stupid Mafia.'

Marco began to explain the situation again. It all sounded exactly like how it had sounded over the various phone calls and messages that the pair of them had exchanged while Rex was staying at Eddie's house.

Why can't Marco just put me front and center.

I know the Mafia is different, but it's still a job.

I want a Daddy who would do ANYTHING to protect me...

Rex had just about had enough of listening to Marco when he decided to ask one more question, and this time he was determined to get a proper answer.

'You *promised* me that you would get revenge on Kash for what he did,' Rex said. 'How can I ever trust you enough to know that you won't just break every other promise you've made or will make in the future? Daddies don't break promises to their Littles.'

Rex felt a sudden pang of guilt. He wasn't sure whether he'd gone too far, and he could see a look of genuine torment and upset in Marco's face.

But Marco didn't give Rex any time to say anything else.

'You just don't listen, do you boy?' Marco said. 'If I've said it once, I've said it a thousand times. Killing Kash would put both of our lives in more danger than they are now. It would be madness.'

'Yes, but at least Kash would be gone forever!' Rex shouted, stomping his foot on the floor.

'Okay, that's just about enough for me for one day,' Marco said, shaking his head. 'I have to go out. It's my fight with Aleksei at the MMA gym today. The last fucking thing I need is to do this, but I made a commitment and I intend to see it through.'

'Oh, you'll keep that promise but not your promise to me?' Rex said, rolling his eyes in disbelief.

'The two examples just aren't' comparable, and you know it,' Marco said, seemingly at the point of totally losing his cool. 'Now, stay in the apartment when I'm gone. We can have a proper, grown-up talk when I get back. Hopefully *both* of us will have calmed down by then.'

Rex couldn't bring himself to respond with words.

Instead, Rex blew a raspberry and stormed into the guestroom, slamming the door behind him.

As Rex listened to Marco picking up his gym bag and leaving the apartment, he didn't know what to think.

Everything was so messed up.

Apparently, the senior Mafia bosses had said that Kash wouldn't bother Rex and Marco in the future in exchange for them not messing with him. This just wasn't enough for Rex. He hated Kash with every bone in his body. And he didn't trust Kash for one second… Kash just wasn't the kind of person to stick to a promise.

As the sound of the penthouse door shutting made its way into the guestroom, Rex hauled himself up onto his feet.

'Marco told me to stay here,' Rex said. 'But I've had enough of him. If Marco can break a promise, there's no reason why I have to do what he says either…'

* * *

Rex knew that Marco would be angry with him for going against his orders, but Rex was a Little on a mission.

After waiting a while to make sure that Marco had truly left the penthouse and gone to the MMA gym, Rex began packing up a bag for himself.

Ozzy? Check.

Diapers? Double check.

Cozy romper? Of course.

Rex zipped up his small backpack and made his way out of the apartment. Fortunately for Rex, Marco's security detail must have been getting a coffee or taking a short bathroom break. Ever since the news about Kash came through, the threat level had been significantly reduced but Rex was still glad that he didn't have to go to the effort of persuading the security to allow him to leave.

As Rex made his way down the elevator to the ground floor, he felt his heart beat with a mixture of excitement and trepidation. This felt risky, but it also was something that Rex wanted to do.

Negotiating the apartment building lobby was easy enough. A large group of important looking businessmen were gathered, which made dodging past the door security a piece of cake.

As he stepped out onto the New York City street, Rex took a moment and inhaled. The fresh air represented his freedom, and far from being a Little with the weight of the world on his shoulders, Rex was determined that he was going to have a wonderful time out on his own.

Rex turned his head so that he could see his trusty stuffie Ozzy's head poking out the top of the backpack.

'This is the right thing to do, isn't it?' Rex said, hopefully. 'Thank you, Ozzy, I agree. I think it is *definitely* the right move too.'

Rex giggled to himself as he began to walk down the sidewalk, a cheery grin on his face and feeling more positive than he had in a couple of days.

Marco would be angry when he found out, but that was an issue that could be shelved until later. Marco had promised to take Kash out of the equation, and seeing as he was now saying that wasn't possible, Rex saw no reason why he should hold up to his end of the bargain and stay at the penthouse.

Rex was only going to think about *his* feelings in this moment.

For Rex, it was all about doing something that would make him feel like the happy, fun-loving Little he knew he was deep down.

The other bonus of sneaking out like this was that Rex knew he wouldn't have anyone following him. It was real freedom. In a strange kind of way, it felt like the first bit of true freedom that Rex had experienced since that fateful night with Kash that started this whole nightmare.

Either way, Rex was determined to at least try and have a good time.

And where better to do that than at Rex's favorite place, *The Peachy Playpen?*

Chapter 20

Marco

Marco hadn't wanted to leave things like he did with Rex, but time was against him, and Marco knew that he couldn't miss the fight with Aleksei.

So much time and effort had gone into training for the matchup and the whole ethos of the gym was built around mutual respect, working hard, and staying true to your commitments.

In many ways, the gym mirrored Marco's life in the Mafia. Only slightly less deadly perhaps. Oh, and the MMA gym life didn't involve making heartbreaking decisions that related to Rex either...

I wanted to stay with the boy.

But Rex needs time to think.

And I have a fight to win...

Upon arriving at the gym, Marco attempted to focus his mind. There was no other option but to blank out all thoughts of Rex and focus only on the task at hand.

The gym was packed. *Everyone* was there. Fighters who were competing that day were busy making their final preparations as loud music boomed over the gym's speaker system. Trainers and non-competing fighters watched on with interest, possibly wondering who they might be facing in the next intra-gym tournament.

There was a tangible sense of anticipation and adrenalin in the air.

The atmosphere was truly electric.

It all served to add an extra layer of determination to Marco. This wasn't going to be an easy fight for him. The chances were that Marco would have to fight the best technical fight of his life to beat Aleksei.

Getting the better of Aleksei truly wouldn't be easy. Far from it. Aleksei was younger, bigger, and he had some serious combat skills too.

But Marco was no slouch either. Marco was hoping that his commitment to training and the wisdom that came with age would help him outsmart and ultimately beat his younger opponent.

'You good?' Tyron said, a slightly concerned look on his face as he began to wrap Marco's hands in protective wrap. 'Word travels fast. I heard about your *difficulties*...'

'I'm good,' Marco replied, a steely determination in his voice. 'I'm here for the win, nothing else. I'm ready to rock and fucking roll.'

'That's the spirit,' Tyron replied, flashing a typically positive smile. 'Some people are making Aleksei the favorite. But my money is on you. All the way. You've got this my man.'

'Thank you, I appreciate it,' Marco said, high fiving Tyron.

'Okay, now it's time for your game face,' Tyron said, noting that it was just about time for Marco and Aleksei to go head-to-head in the cage together. 'Heart. Mind. Intensity. This is your fight to win.'

Marco nodded and stepped through the cage door.

Across on the other side was Aleksei. He looked in supreme shape, as he always did. Even with his partying lifestyle, Aleksei was one of those guys who could still look like a million dollars. In part, it was probably down to his relative youth. Certainly, Marco wasn't unable to stay out all night and then train the next day.

'Ready to lose?' Aleksei called out from across the octagon. 'Your ass is mine, old man.'

Marco shook his head.

This kid thinks he's the cat's pajamas.

And that's going to be his downfall.

It's time to show him how Marco Santino fights for real...

The starter buzzer sounded and the two men moved toward one another in the center of the octagon. Marco held out his fist for a customary fist bump, but Aleksei refused.

Aleksei may have thought he was being clever, but all this minor disrespect did was focus Marco's mind even more on what he needed to do to win.

After a few moments of testing each other out and figuring the distances between them, the two men clashed in the center of the octagon. Fists were flying and so were kicks and elbows too. This may have been an intra-gym tournament fight, but Marco and Aleksei were going after each other like it was a world title fight with millions of dollars and the championship belt on the line.

After a pulsating first round, both fighters retreated to their corners, ready for water and words of advice from their respective trainers.

'How's it looking?' Marco said, taking a seat and sipping on some water.

'Looks good, you're definitely in this fight,' Tyron said. 'Keep working, keep making him waste shots. You'll tire him out, I know you will. Remember, you have the superior fighter IQ.'

'Got it,' Marco said, slowly working through his breathing techniques to slow his heart rate and get rid of as much fatigue as he could.

All the while, Aleksei hadn't even bothered to sit in his corner. Instead, he was calling out to his friends in the audience, bragging and hollering about how he had gone easy on Marco in the first round.

'Big fucking mistake,' Marco said, looking at Tyron and exchanging a wry smile. 'I think this sonofabitch is ready to face the hardest round of his life.'

As the two men met in the center of the octagon for the second round, Aleksei swung wildly not once, not twice, but three times. Each punch missed the target due to Marco's fast reaction times.

Aleksei let out a yelp of frustration.

'Not getting tired are you?' Marco said, smiling and leaving his chin dangling for Aleksei to take another swing at.

'*Argh*! Screw you, old man!' Aleksei bellowed, yet again missing with a series of punches and kicks.

Marco then threw a few shots of his own, each one connecting with Aleksei. The temptation was to keep on going on the attack, but Marco held back and offered Aleksei a chance to retaliate.

This time, Marco held his guard close to his body and allowed Aleksei to land a series of blows. The kicks weren't scoring any points as they were all landing on Marco's arms or gloves.

Marco could see Aleksei's frustration. And his tiredness too.

He's ready to go.

His gas tank is almost empty.

I just need him to unleash one more barrage...

Just as Marco wanted, Aleksei unleashed a huge series of punches, each one with the sole aim of knocking Marco down. But by this point, Aleksei was fatigued and his punches had far less power. He had burned himself out and it wasn't even the end of the second round yet.

This was Marco's moment.

Seeing that Aleksei was breathing hard and looking worn out, Marco pummeled his rival with body shots, winding him hard and sending Aleksei staggering backward.

'Take him down!' Tyron shouted from outside the cage. But Marco was already well on the way to enacting his trainer's wishes.

Three stiff jabs to Aleksei's guard broke his defense, and one huge left hook to follow up sent an exhausted Aleksei to the canvas. Marco charged to finish him off, but the referee could see that Aleksei was done and stepped in and called the fight off.

Marco had won.

The crowd cheered and applauded what had been an explosive match up. Marco looked down on a bruised and tired Aleksei. The truth was that some of Aleksei's shots had hurt Marco, but Aleksei just hadn't had the right game plan.

'Good fight,' Marco said, offering his hand to Aleksei.

'Fuck off,' Aleksei said, standing on wobbly feet. 'You got lucky. Don't think you've heard the last of this. I'll spring a surprise on you when you least expect it...'

Marco couldn't believe what he was hearing. This was totally uncalled for. The look of anger on Aleksei's face was like that of a spoilt child. But it was also worrying that Aleksei seemed to be implying there would be a beef outside of the gym walls.

'Security, get this asshole out of here,' Tyron said, anger in his voice. 'It was a fair fight. We fight hard in this gym. We show honor. And we certainly don't act like *that* in defeat.'

'Don't worry,' Marco said, turning to Tyron as several burly gym members dragged Aleksei out of the gym. 'Aleksei knows he's in the wrong. It's just a question of when he'll be willing to admit that to himself.'

'You fought a hell of a fight,' Tyron said. 'How about sticking around to watch the other fights? We can grab a beer afterward?'

'Thank you, but I've got a certain someone I need to see,' Marco said, his thoughts now back on Rex. 'This fight has given me some real clarity on some things. Catch you in training next week, Ty.'

Marco and Tyron embraced.

It felt great to win the fight, but as far as Marco was concerned it was time to head back home.

Marco had a very special boy who he needed to make things right with.

* * *

Marco raced back home without even taking the time to have a shower. Fortunately, he was being driven back by his own personal driver so didn't have to worry about stinking out an unsuspecting Uber driver's car.

On arrival back at the penthouse, Marco felt determined to make everything okay with Rex. There simply had to be an answer to the Kash situation that would at least go some way to pleasing everyone.

I don't know what I'll say.

I just know I have to make it right.

Rex is too important to lose. He's means way too much to me...

However as Marco entered the penthouse, a sinking feeling came over him. There was an eerie silence in the air. Somehow, Marco just knew that Rex wasn't at home.

'Rex?' Marco called out. 'Where are you?'

Marco went from room to room, but there was no sign of Rex. After checking each and every room, Marco looped back round to the bedroom.

'Oh no, what have you done, boy?' Marco bellowed.

Marco saw that Rex's stuff had been moved around, and that Ozzy wasn't there, and some other items were missing too.

Rex was gone.

But where?

And, worst of all, Marco didn't know if Rex was safe or even if he would ever see him again. Marco had arrived back home with every intention of making things right. But now it looked like that chance may have gone. Marco's only hope was that his chance to have his happy ever after with Rex hadn't gone... *for good.*

Chapter 21

Rex

The journey to the *Peachy Playpen* was meant to be fun, but on the way there Rex found himself constantly being spooked by looks from strangers, sudden noises, or any vehicle that remotely resembled a blacked out SUV.

This wasn't how it was supposed to go.

Rex was taking back control of his life, having fun again, doing what he wanted to do and not bothering with Marco's rules. This should have been a fun walk across toward one of Rex's favorite places.

Kash could be anywhere.

He could be watching me right now.

No, don't be a silly Little. Just get to the Peachy and have fun...

Rex pushed down any bad thoughts and continued along with his journey, even if he did avoid any of the shortcuts that took him down less well-populated areas.

'We'll be there soon, Ozzy,' Rex said, stopping to take his stuffie out of his backpack. 'I'll just carry you like this. You can better keep me company that way.'

Rex thought back to how much fun him and Ozzy, and his Little friends too, had before the whole Kash disaster had struck. Life felt like one big, never-ending party. Rex would work hard at the *Peachy Playpen*, but it didn't even really feel like work because he enjoyed it so much.

In fact, Rex realized that his perfect job at the *Peachy Playpen* was similar to the situation his father had been in at his own work. Rex's father worked at a timber yard for over twenty-five years, right up until he passed away. Rex would often ask his father what he liked most about working at the timber yard, and his father would reply that each and every day was a new challenge, an opportunity to work hard, and a great time with his friends and co-workers.

A club for Littles and a timberyard might not have had much in common as workplaces, but Rex felt exactly the same about his job as his father had about his.

I miss him.

Poppa would have known what to do in this situation.

There's no way he would have made me hide away...

With thoughts of his father filling his mind, Rex felt extra-determined to vanquish Kash from his mind and head to the *Peachy Playpen* and have the best time he possibly could.

As Rex stood at the crossing and waited for the lights to change, he smiled a big smile. His father would be proud of him for refusing to give up on a life of fun and being open hearted.

It was a shame the way things seemed to have worked out between Rex and Marco, but Rex felt happy at least that he was taking his first steps back to being his old self.

All that was left was walk a couple more blocks and enter through the doors of his favorite Little club in the whole wide world.

The *Peachy Playpen* was as busy as ever, and Rex took a moment to take the atmosphere in as he stepped inside for the first time in what felt like an eternity.

'It's good to be back,' Rex said, brining Ozzy in for an extra tight snuggle. 'I've missed this place.'

With the sound of nursery rhyme pop remixes playing over the speaker system and a big bunch of Little dancing in the main play area, Rex felt himself relax into the vibe.

Rex hadn't told either Eddie or Mac that he was coming out of fear that their Daddies would find out and then tell Marco. The last thing that Rex wanted was for an angry Marco to show up and either shout at him or make him go back to the penthouse.

So as much as it would have been nice to hang out with Eddie or Mac, Rex knew that it wasn't to be on this occasion. Instead, Rex was determined to do what he always did in the past. Rex decided to have fun, speak to new people, and simply see where the moment took him.

Being spontaneous and fun was all about branching out into the world with a smile and a having fun. Rex felt sure that this is exactly what his father would have told him to do, and with that in mind he made his way toward the locker room.

'The sooner I'm in my diaper and romper, the better!' Rex said, a delighted squeal in his voice as he skipped toward the locker room.

After a quick change, Rex was back out in the playroom wearing his cozy romper with the security of a thick, fluffy diaper underneath. He may not have been in Littlespace just yet, but Rex felt like he could be on his way soon enough.

With a group of three friendly looking Littles dancing away on the large playmat, Rex wandered over and began dancing around them.

'Hey, come and join us!' the Little with the blonde hair and tiger-striped romper suit said. 'This is all of our first times here. It's great. Have you been here before?'

'You could say that!' Rex giggled. 'I actually work here. Well, I normally do. Anyway, my name's Rex.'

The three other Littles introduced themselves and soon enough they were all dancing and giggling away as they, and their stuffies too of course, sang along to the songs.

'*Phew*, I think I need a drink,' the blonde haired Little said. 'My name's Alex by the way. I've just moved here from LA.'

'I'm Rex,' Rex replied, a big smile on his face. 'Do you want to share my juice box?'

Alex and Rex giggled as they took turns to take sips from Rex's mango and strawberry juice box. It felt so good to make not just one, but three new friends so quickly. This was truly what the spirit of the *Peachy Playpen* was all about, and it was exactly what Rex had missed in recent times.

'Shall we go and play in the ball pit?' Alex said, his blue eyes twinkling with excitement. 'Last one in is a rotten tomato!'

The Littles squealed with delight and ran toward the large, deep ball pit with looks of pure joy on their faces. Rex managed to get himself to the front of the line and practically threw himself into the plastic balls as if he was diving into a swimming pool.

'*Yaaay*! I won!' Rex cried out triumphantly as he popped up from beneath the plastic balls. 'Ball pit fight!'

Rex began to throw all the different colored balls along with his new friends. The Littles were laughing and having the time of their lives until suddenly Rex dropped his ball and stared into the distance.

'Hey, Rex, what's up?' Alex said, a look of surprise on his face. 'I didn't throw my ball too hard, did I?'

'N-n-n-n-no,' Rex said, his voice trembling and a look of sheer panic coming over him. 'It's... *him*. He's... *here*.'

Suddenly, the voices of Rex's new friends just seemed to fade into the background. All Rex could focus on was the sight of Kash standing in the lobby.

Kash was being loud and showing off, just like he did on the first time that Rex met him. With his all-black outfit and flashy gold jewelry, Kash looked like he was trying to make an impression.

Rex shuddered at the very thought that Kash would try and take someone else from the *Peachy Playpen* out to party like he did with Rex.

But Rex knew too that it was only a matter of time, seconds maybe, before Kash turned and looked over toward him in the ball pit.

Why did he have to come here?

I was having such a fun time.

I feel scared. I shouldn't have come. I need my Daddy...

Chapter 22

Marco

The music played in the background, a classic of Italian opera that set the tone perfectly for the restaurant. Marco wasn't an expert in opera by any means, but he knew that every time he came to *Dante's Kitchen*, he would be in for an aural treat.

The wine at *Dante's Kitchen* was never anything less than the finest, most traditionally sourced and aged red wine in the whole city. Marco was more of a whiskey drinker, but he couldn't deny that his good friend Dante had a brilliant selection of wine to choose from.

Marco was at *Dante's Kitchen* along with Dante and Rocco too. The three Daddies were sitting at the back of the restaurant on Dante's personal table, its slightly raised position offering them a view across the dining area and providing a perfect vantage point to spot any sudden threats.

Of course, no one was expecting anything to go down.

Dante had excellent security on the door, and round the back too. Plus there had always been an understanding between the crime families that any feuds should be dealt with away from the public eye.

'See, I'll make a wine convert of you yet,' Dante said, noticing how much Marco was enjoying his glass of 1973 red. 'But we're not here to talk about fine wine, are we?'

Dante, Rocco, and Marco exchanged a knowing look.

'No, we're not,' Marco said, a gravely serious tone in his voice. 'What we're talking about is pretty much as serious as it gets. We're talking about going against the elders.'

Even speaking this out loud was enough to make Marco take a deep intake of breath. He could see on the faces of Rocco and Dante that this was a huge deal for them too.

It was important to Marco that neither one of his friends were doing this for the wrong reasons, simply out of loyalty to him. They had their own boys to look after, and Marco wanted to ensure that they were fully committed.

'I'll say this one more time, guys,' Marco said, looking at Rocco and Dante in turn as he spoke. 'If you want to back out and protect yourselves and your boys, I understand without reservation. This is dangerous. It's about as dangerous a move as you can make in our business.'

Marco paused. He wanted to give Rocco and Dante a moment to think. But it turned out that neither of Marco's friends needed any time at all to consider their response...

'We've got your back,' Dante said, smiling.

'Always,' Rocco added. 'Thank you for asking, but don't worry about us old sonsofbitches. We came into this game together, near enough. And if we have to, we'll go out together.'

Marco nodded. He felt a deep connection to his fellow Mafia Daddies, and to hear them speak like this was significant. Having lost his parents so young, Marco had never really experienced what family felt like. But in Rocco and Dante, Marco felt like he had two true brothers in all but biology.

'And now that's settled, let's talk business,' Dante said, taking a sip of his wine. 'I think we can do this in a way without the elder bosses finding out. That won't be easy, but it's not impossible.'

'They'll know it's me,' Marco said. 'Whatever we do, they'll see through the play. You don't get to become one of the untouchable higher-ups by not being able to read any play.'

'Maybe, maybe not,' Rocco said. 'We've been through enough situations together where the odds were stacked against us. Let's get real, we're probably more on top of our game than our bosses are. They're old. We're... *mature*. There's a difference.'

Marco could see what Rocco was saying.

If I can plan a complex bank heist, I can work this puzzle.

There has to be a way.

I just need time to see the right play...

But before Marco and his friends could spend any time mapping out a possible solution to the problem, they were suddenly joined at the table by Cal, one of their most reliable spies.

'Cal, to what do we owe this honor?' Marco said, thinking this was perhaps to do with the bank heist he had been planning. 'Any updates on the insider we've been working at the bank?'

'Marco, you may want to take a big drink first,' Cal said, a nervous look on his face. 'This is to do with Kash Vialli.'

The three Mafia Daddies were immediately in high-alert mode.

Cal was a reliable and highly skilled spy. If he was bringing news of Kash, then it was almost certainly not going to be good news, and it was without doubt going to be accurate.

'Talk,' Marco said, his body stiffening with tension.

'Kash was seen over on Duke Avenue,' Cal said, his voice clear and calm. 'We trailed him. He was rolling with a couple of other guys, known associates. He goes down Duke, then over onto Malpas, then onto-'

'Fuck, he was headed for the *Peachy Playpen*,' Marco said, immediately standing up from the table. 'I need to move and fucking move *right now*.'

'Wait, there's more,' Cal said, putting his arm on Marco's shoulder. 'Kash went into the Peachy Playpen and came out with a boy. Sandy blonde, romper suit, dangly earring, a strawberry or something similar.'

'That's Rex,' Marco said, his jaw clenching and a look of intense focus coming over him. 'That motherfucker has got Rex.'

'Kash put him in his car, and we lost him,' Cal said. 'But... we know where Kash's new hideout is over on this side of town. I'll message you the location now.'

Marco's mind was racing with possibilities.

Kash was a thug and a killer. He had none of the loyalty or honor that came with being a real Mafia man. Kash was an outsider looking to become a face in the criminal underworld.

Worse, Kash also seemed to take a delight in tormenting and hurting people. Just because Rex was connected to the Mafia via Marco, it wouldn't stop Kash from hurting the boy.

Marco knew that he had to move, and he had to move quickly.

Suddenly, the idea of planning out some kind of operation to take Kash out without the elder bosses finding out was out of the window. This situation needed resolving now, no matter the cost.

Fortunately for Marco, he had his loyal Mafia Daddies with him.

'Marco, you go and kill that sonofabitch,' Rocco said. 'Dante and I will give you an alibi should you need one.'

'And you can count me in on that too, friend,' Cal said, his square jaw clenching and his green eyes complimenting his short, strawberry blonde hair. 'I may not be official Mafia, and I'm not Italian blood, but I've got you on this *all* the fucking way, Marco.'

'Take my Porsche,' Rocco said, tossing Marco his keys. 'All black, turbo charged. You know the one.'

Marco nodded.

There was no time for any pleasantries. Marco left the restaurant and hopped into Rocco's Porsche.

It was time to find Kash and put this whole sorry affair to bed once and for all. Marco knew there was a chance that he might not make it out alive, but that was a chance he was more than willing to take.

As Marco fired up the Porsche's turbo charged engine, he pulled away onto the New York city streets and felt his brain engage into Mafia business mode. Yes, Marco loved Rex with all of his heart. But Marco couldn't allow himself to become wrapped up in emotion. What Marco needed was to treat this as any other piece of work.

Clear your thoughts.

Fix on the objective.

You're shooting to kill.

As Marco weaved in and out of the traffic with precision and skill, he felt his body relaxing into the moment. Many people crumbled under pressure, but Marco had been in far too many high octane moments during bank heists to allow that to happen.

A situation like this was part of Marco's bread and butter. Not many men climbed as high or lasted as long in the Mafia as Marco had. His success wasn't down to luck either.

Just as he had defeated Aleksei in the MMA octagon, Marco was going to utilize every drop of his personal experience to take Kash on. Kash was young, fearless, and acted like he had nothing to lose. In many ways, these were Kash's strengths. But Marco was going to use these so-called strengths against

Kash and turn them into weaknesses, just like he had done with Aleksei.

The mission was clear, and Marco knew he had no room to maneuver. It was now or never, and failure simply was not an option on the table.

Rex was in danger. His life was potentially on the line that very second as Marco swung the Porsche around another corner that took him closer to Kash's new hideout.

Marco knew what he needed to do.

It was time to make sure that Kash could never, *ever* hurt anyone again.

Chapter 23

Rex

Rex had never felt so scared in his life. Despite trying to hide from Kash at the *Peachy Playpen*, it wasn't long before Kash and his men found him cowering behind the big plastic tree in the corner of the woodland play area.

The look on Kash's face had been one of pure evil, the kind of manic smile and spite-filled eyes that would pass Kash off as a villain from a superhero movie. The one difference from a superhero movie being that Rex had no idea whether his ultimate hero would be able to save him or not.

Kash had threated Rex that if he didn't come quietly, then he would simply beat him up on the spot and drag him out. Rex knew that he had no chance against Kash and his men, and he also feared that if he shouted for help he would just make things a hundred times worse.

The problem with dealing with Kash was, as Marco had said over and over again, was that Kash didn't have any values or morals. Kash was wild and couldn't be trusted to stick to even the most basic standards of decency.

Being face to face with Kash was such a scary prospect that Rex had simply done exactly as Kash ordered him to. Even the concerned looks from Rex's new Little friends as he walked out of the *Peachy Playpen* with Kash hadn't been able to provoke Rex into reaching out for help.

Rex was now sitting in the back of Kash's SUV and travelling across town. The traffic was pretty bad, and although this meant that it bought Rex some time, it also felt like it was simply delaying the inevitable.

Maybe I should have run?

I could have screamed and hoped that someone would have helped?

Urgh. I just want... Marco. I need my Daddy.

As the SUV came to a standstill in a sudden bottleneck of traffic, Rex looked up and caught Kash's eye in the rearview mirror. Despite looking away as quickly as he could, it was too late. Kash had seen Rex looking in his direction and now wanted to play.

Except, this was a game that Rex had zero interested in partaking in...

'Hey, why so shy?' Kash snarled, turning around from the passenger seat up front. 'Show me that pretty face of yours...'

'Go away, I don't want to talk to you,' Rex said, blurting his words out as bravely as he could manage. 'Why do you have to do this? I never did anything to you.'

'I'm doing this because I *can* do this,' Kash said, a wicked laugh following his words. ''I'm Kash Vialli. People need to understand that I do what I want, when I want, and *however* I want.'

'But... why can't you just leave me alone?' Rex replied, finding the courage from within him to speak up and push back on Kash's claims. 'Just stop the car and let me get out. I... I... I'll even tell my Daddy to not come for you.'

Rex immediately knew he had made a mistake.

The look on Kash's face was one of pure rage. The very mention of Marco had seemingly blackened Kash's mood in a way that was scary and left Rex worried about his own safety more than ever.

'Marco Santino?' Kash snarled. 'That old man is the past. I'm the future. You call him your Daddy? Just wait until I give you the spanking you really need. You freaks don't know what real punishment is. But don't worry, you'll soon learn all about that.'

Rex was stunned. He couldn't speak, his mind was all over the place trying to work out exactly what Kash meant.

'You silly boy,' Kash said, moving from the front seat and sitting next to Rex in the rear of the SUV. 'I know what kind of things you Littles like, and I'm ready to put my own very special Kash Vialli spin on things. Whether you like it or not!'

'You're not my Daddy!' Rex said, tears filling in his eyes. 'Only my Daddy can punish me! Not you! You'll never be able to!'

Rex was worried that his mouth was running away with itself and making things worse. Yet on the other hand, the situation felt so desperate that Rex saw no other option but to defend himself until he couldn't defend himself any longer.

As Kash continued to taunt Rex, call him names, and even suggest the kinds of punishments he would dole out, Rex found his mind going into a slightly calmer, more analytical mode.

Are the doors locked?

Could I jump out?

Would I be quick enough to escape?

But Rex wasn't used to making the kind of escape plans that his brain was desperately trying to conjure. And it must have been obvious to Kash what Rex was thinking too.

Before Rex could get any further in planning what could be a heroic escape, Kash reached into the front of the car and came back with a pair of metal handcuffs in his hands.

'Silly little fool,' Kash said, roughly putting Rex's hands in the cuffs. 'This isn't the first time I've done this. Or haven't you worked that out yet?'

'*Aww*, the handcuffs are too tight!' Rex pleaded, his attempts to wriggle free not going down well with Kash.

'Stop moving or I'll make them tighter,' Kash shouted. 'And just in case you were wondering, the doors are all locked anyway. Now be a nice, polite boy or I'll gag you too. Hell, I might do that anyway, just for a laugh.'

Rex suddenly went quiet and simply shook his head, his eyes pleading for mercy. Rex hated being in this position. He may have been a Little with a submissive streak, but Rex had absolutely no desire whatsoever to submit to such an awful, horrible man like Kash.

In fact, Kash was about as far from a Daddy as Rex could ever imagine. Kash didn't take control of people through respect and loving discipline. Kash took control through bullying and being mean. Rex hated Kash with every bone in his body.

'You don't scare me!' Rex said, angrily spitting out the words and stomping his feet on the SUV's plush interior floor. 'You're nothing but a big, mean, loser-butt!'

'And you just made a big mistake,' Kash laughed, shaking his head. 'Here, see how this fits...'

With that, Kash reached forward into the front of the SUV again and came back with a ball gag. Rex tried to move his head and resist it, but Kash simply held him by the neck and made it clear that refusal would only lead to pain.

'Now, finally it looks like the traffic's clearing up,' Kash smirked. 'Here's to a quieter second half of the journey. No more whining and talking shit from stupid little Rex.'

Kash and the thug driving the SUV laughed together as Rex did his best to hold things together. The ball gag in his mouth was uncomfortable and felt humiliating. Rex didn't want to cry any more in front of Kash, and did everything in his power to not let any more tears flow from his eyes.

Rex began to realize that going against his Daddy's wishes and leaving the apartment like that was a huge mistake. In hindsight, Rex knew that going to the *Peachy Playpen* was a crazy thing to do, no matter how sad or frustrated Rex had felt at the time.

Why was I so silly?

I should have known that Daddy knew best.

He's a Mafia man, I'm just... me.

As the SUV began to increase speed as the traffic cleared, Rex realized that he overreacted to Marco not being able to go after Kash as he had first promised. Of course Marco would have done it *if* he was able to, but that option had been taken off the table.

And the way things were shaping up, perhaps it was even true that what Rex had really needed all along was a Daddy to protect him rather than avenge him.

With these thoughts in his head and panic and uncertainty coursing around his body, Rex closed his eyes and thought back to the first time him and Marco had met. The chemistry. The feeling of being safe. The connection. All of these things meant so much to Rex.

All Rex could do was hope and pray that Marco could come to his rescue. The alternatives were just way too scary to even contemplate. Rex needed his Daddy, and he needed him *fast*.

Chapter 24

Marco

The Porsche roared around the corner and Marco brought it to a slow crawl, the engine rumbling as he brought the speed right down. It was a run-down neighborhood, all shabby storefronts and questionable looking people hanging out on the street corners.

Marco pulled down a side alley and turned the car engine off. There wasn't any time to waste, but Marco went through the same process he had done for years before a big job or life endangering strike.

Put simply, Marco *breathed*.

In and then out, in and then out, Marco slowed his breathing down and felt a sense of total concentration come over him. Marco had learned this technique from the man who took him under his wing many years ago.

Alphonso was a tough old Mafia guy, straight from the old school. But the knowledge that Alphonso imparted on Marco had served him so well over the last couple of decades that he wasn't about to forget it now, in the moment where Marco needed it the most.

Adrenalin may have been pumping around Marco's body, and his senses were all set to high alert. But Marco knew that the best way of approaching this moment was to focus his mind, control his emotions as best he could, and then walk into Kash's hideout with a controlled sense of purpose on one thing, and one thing only.

This is the place.

Kash is here.

And he's got my boy...

Marco double-checked the information from his spy, but instinctively he knew he was at the right address.

Marco's instincts had proven right over many years of Mafia work, and this was simply another time where instinct would have to override anything else. Maybe it didn't make sense to go into the building alone, and surely the odds would be stacked against Marco depending on how many men Kash had in there with him.

But Marco didn't have a choice.

This was about protecting his boy and then exacting a final revenge on Kash. There was no backing out, no half-measures, this was a showdown where only one of them would come out alive. Potentially, it was a situation where neither Marco nor Kash would survive, but Marco was willing to take that chance if it meant that Rex would finally be safe and able to live a happy life again.

'Okay, Santino,' Marco said, adjusting his black tie in the rearview mirror. 'It's time to go to work.'

With that, Marco got out of the Porsche and walked up the alley and back onto the main street. Marco looked around to see if he could spot any of Kash's men who might already be on the lookout.

'Looks clear,' Marco said, under his breath.

Marco had figured that Kash would surely anticipate him coming after Rex. Even if Kash knew that Marco had been forbidden from coming after him, Marco was in no doubt that Kash would at the very least be on high alert for Marco to show up.

Marco thought back to the memory of his parents being murdered. Marco's father was part of the Mafia life and would have known full well that one day he might die at the hand of someone else's bullets. But for the assassin to take out Marco's mother too, that had been truly despicable.

Marco's mother wasn't Mafia, other than through her marriage. It wasn't right. Just how it wasn't right that Rex was being used by Kash as some kind of power play.

We keep civilians out of the business.

We show honor, respect, and class.

And now it's time to teach Kash a one-time lesson in all the above...

With a look of steely focus on his face, Marco walked toward the building where Kash was purportedly hiding out.

Despite its shabby exterior, upon stepping inside, Marco could see that it was some kind of underground bar. Clearly, the New York City licensing committee had *no idea* that this place existed.

With its velvet seats, ominous neon lights and clientele who looked like they were on any number of illicit substances, Marco could see that he was in the front facing part of this underground bar.

There was no way that Kash would hang out here, up front and on full display. There had to be another part of the bar, a place reserved for the VIPs and the people who no doubt wanted to keep their identity a secret.

There were almost certainly private rooms too, places where people could go to get up to all manner of things. Marco wasn't a prude, he'd seen many things over the years and didn't judge people for their choices as long as no one else was harmed.

But this was Kash Vialli's place.

The chances of everything being safe and ethical were slim to none.

As Marco continued to look around, he noticed a heavy, deep-purple curtain that was draped across a segment of the rear wall. But before Marco could investigate for himself, he heard the sound of a female voice, suddenly all up close and personal.

'Can I get you a drink, sir' the waitress said as she approached Marco.

'I'm looking for a *private* drink,' Marco said. 'Somewhere I won't be disturbed.'

The waitress paused before responding, an uncertain look on her face. The waitress's uncertainty didn't last for very long however as Marco flashed a hundred dollars from his metal wallet.

'I need the *most* private place here,' Marco said, smiling.

'Of course, sir,' the waitress replied, deftly taking Marco's money and walking toward the very same deep-purple curtain that Marco had spotted only moments earlier.

The waitress pulled the curtain back to reveal a locked door. Using her fingerprint for access, the waitress opened the door and stepped to one side to allow Marco access.

'Have fun,' the waitress said, smiling as she walked away.

'Fun? We'll see about that,' Marco growled, his heart beginning to thump as he sensed he was closer than ever to finding Rex.

The heavy metal security door shut behind Marco and he stepped forward into a narrow corridor, shut doors on either side all the way up. This was definitely a place where people came to do things in private, but that wasn't the focus of Marco's attention in that moment.

Marco was on a mission to find his boy.

And with a small bar area at the top of the corridor, Marco knew he had to move with subtlety in order to not get spotted by either Kash's thugs or Kash himself.

Marco worked his way up the corridor, opening the doors as he went along, but only enough to peer inside enough to confirm whether Rex or Kash were in there.

The low thud of deep techno music made its way down from the bar area, but it wasn't anywhere near distracting Marco from his cause. Marco's mind was fixed on what he needed to do, and nothing or no one could distract him from that.

Find Rex.

Kill Kash.

Get the hell out of dodge.

Suddenly, Marco felt a hand on his shoulder. Ready for any trouble, Marco spun around to face whoever it was placing their hands on him.

'You?' Marco said, his voice stern and his mind racing with possibilities.

'Yeah, it's me,' Aleksei replied. 'Don't you know it's rude to walk in on someone's private room?'

Marco tried to gauge Aleksei's mood. He seemed perturbed, even a little bit angry. It was likely that Aleksei only needed the slightest excuse to try and seek revenge for his loss in the MMA tournament. And maybe Marco had just unwittingly given Aleksei exactly what he wanted...

'Listen, I'm sorry for barging in on you,' Marco said. 'No disrespect meant on my part. I know we haven't got along in the past, but you know I don't move like that.'

Marco delivered his words firmly but with sincerity. He knew that Aleksei could be a hot head, but he was from a good mobster family who would have at least attempted to teach Aleksei about respect.

'*Hmmm*, well, whatever,' Aleksei said. 'But anyway, at least tell me what brings you here?'

'Kash Vialli's got my boy,' Marco said. 'He's a low life piece of shit, and I'm here to make him pay. There are lines you simply do not cross, and Kash has crossed at least half a dozen of them with me, and with my associates too.'

'This is Vialli's place?' Aleksei said. 'I had no fucking idea. I was invited here by... a friend. I know enough about Kash Vialli to know I can't stand him.'

'Okay, so you get why I'm here,' Marco said. 'Now, if you'll let me move on, I'm working on a ticking clock here...'

'Let you move on?' Aleksei said. 'I don't think so.'

Marco was ready to reach for his gun. Time was of the essence and he couldn't accept being held up a moment longer, especially not if Aleksei was about to cause more trouble.

'Listen, what happened in the gym, stays in the gym,' Marco said, his hand on his gun.

'Yeah, it does,' Aleksei replied. 'And us MMA guys stick the fuck together. Especially when it comes to a common enemy like Kash. He can't mess with your boy either. That shit ain't right. I'm coming with you.'

Marco nodded.

This may have been a surprising turn of events, but Marco wasn't going to turn down Aleksei's offer of help. Ideally,

Marco wouldn't have come alone, and knowing that he had a highly capable fighter alongside him was an unexpected bonus.

Anything that would help get Rex back was a positive.

'Marco Santino and Aleksei Ivanov, partners?' Aleksei said, a mischievous grin on his face. 'Just wait 'till the guys at the gym here about this.'

'Enough talk,' Marco said, rolling his eyes. 'It's time to take down Kash's men. No mercy.'

'No mercy,' Aleksei replied. 'Just how I like it.'

Marco and Aleksei proceeded to work their way up through the rooms, taking down Kash's men as they appeared. Working as a team, Marco and Aleksei were too fast, strong, and skilled in one-on-one combat for any of Kash's thugs.

It was almost *too* easy.

But the longer it went without locating either Kash or Rex, the more Marco felt like they were working toward some kind of final showdown. Marco knew that Kash liked having his thugs around him, so as they approached the final door there was a feeling that this was about to be a big moment.

'You ready?' Marco said.

'I was born ready,' Aleksei replied. 'Us Ivanovs fear nothing or no one. You should know that by now.'

'Damn right I do,' Marco said, feeling a dull ache in his rib cage from where Aleksei had landed some hefty blows in their fight together. 'On my count. Three. Two. One-'

Chapter 25

Rex

Rex felt horrible. Being in a small room with Kash and two of his righthand men was a bad feeling all round, and the fact that they were in some kind of sleazy private club just made things a ton worse.

At least Kash had taken Rex's gag out of his mouth, but even that didn't come without its downside. Kash was now expecting Rex to talk to him...

'Come on, tell me this isn't the coolest hangout in town?' Kash said, sneering as he sipped on an expensive looking bottle of champagne. 'Come on, relax. I thought you liked to have fun and party?'

Rex didn't want to even open his mouth, let alone speak to Kash.

He's everything I hate.

Mean, rude, and a bully.

Kash is the worst person in the whole world...

'I don't want to do *anything* with you!' Rex said, trying his best to sound as brave as was possible under the circumstances. 'I do too like to have fun. But only with kind, fun people and not absolute butt-stinkers like you!'

Rex felt his heart beating very hard indeed. He could see that his words had embarrassed Kash in front of his thugs.

It might not have been a wise move to annoy Kash like that, but at this point Rex simply didn't care anymore. Rex was sick of living in fear of Kash. Not only had Kash caused Rex a ton of pain and hurt, but Kash had also managed to put a huge dent in Rex's relationship with Marco.

But as good as it felt to let loose and tell Kash what he thought of him, Rex was suddenly aware that there might be consequences too...

'You are a stupid little fool,' Kash said, taking a huge gulp of champagne straight from the bottle. 'You're a rude, spoilt, pathetic little freak in fact!'

Rex might have burst into tears at a comment like that before. But he suddenly felt stronger and more resilient than he ever had done. Kash could say what he liked, but Rex knew that he was a good person.

Being with a Mafia man like Marco must have toughened Rex up and given him the resilience he needed to not be scared so much around bullies. Instead of cowering away, Rex sat up straight and looked Kash directly in the eyes.

'I'm not scared of you,' Rex said, a defiant tone in his voice. 'My Daddy taught me a lot. And one thing I learned was that if you're confident in yourself then you don't need to fear others.'

Rex felt proud for taking a stand, but Kash didn't exactly see it the same way. In fact, nothing could have been further from the truth...

'Ha! Oh my God, what a loser,' Kash sneered, looking at his thugs and shrieking with laughter. 'Your Daddy? Well, where is he now? Maybe he did teach you some stuff, but that won't count for anything when I'm through with you, you little dork.'

'I'm still not scared!' Rex said, thumping his fists down on the plush seating. 'You'll never scare me again!

'Okay, I was going to take my time and have fun with this,' Kash said. 'But this freak is too annoying. Someone pass me my gun right this fucking second...'

Rex felt himself go pale.

For all that it felt good to stand up to Kash, he didn't want to die for it. Suddenly Rex wished that he'd kept his mouth firmly zipped shut.

'Okay, now it's time to pay the price for talking shit to Kash Vialli,' Kash said, taking a metal handgun from one of his thugs and aiming it at Rex. 'Goodnight, Rex...'

Rex was about to say a prayer when suddenly the door to the room swung open and in burst Marco. And by the looks of it, he had a friend with him...

'Daddy!' Rex squealed. 'Aleksei?'

'Long story... will explain later,' Marco said, lunging forward and kicking Kash's gun right out of his hand. 'Got some business to handle first.'

'Yay, Daddy!' Rex cried, backing himself up against the wall as chaos reigned supreme in the small room.

Rex watched on as Marco and Aleksei set to work on fighting Kash and his two henchmen. It might have been three against two, but Marco and Aleksei were more than capable of picking up the slack of being a man down.

Rex wasn't sure exactly why or how Marco and Aleksei were working together, but he certainly wasn't complaining. The sight of Aleksei throwing kick after kick into the mid-section of the biggest thug was a sight to behold.

'Go get 'em!' Rex cheered, although his smile suddenly disappeared when he saw Kash sneak up behind Aleksei and hit him from behind.

'Not so fucking fast,' Marco growled, pulling Kash back into a one-on-one fight with him. 'I've taken down one of your thugs, now it's just you and me. And one of us ain't leaving this room alive.'

'And I suppose you think that's me, huh?' Kash grinned, a sly look on his face as he dodged out of Marco's way and went to grab at something from behind the sofa.

'Another gun?' Marco said. 'Let's see how long you hold on to that one.'

But while Marco had been able to kick Kash's other gun out of his hand, that definitely wasn't an option now. It wasn't a gun that Kash was holding in his hand this time, it was a machete.

'Daddy! Be careful!' Rex cried, now in a state of panic as he saw Kash wielding the long, wide, and super-sharp looking blade. 'Aleksei, help my Daddy!'

'No, Aleksei, I'm cool,' Marco said, noticing that Aleksei had taken out the other thug. 'I've got this.'

'One hundred percent you've got this,' Aleksei said, towering over the fallen thug and watching as Kash and Rex circled each other. 'This punk doesn't know how bad a mistake he's making.'

'Shut your mouth, Russian,' Kash said, his eyes wild and his voice now totally manic as he swung the machete from side to side. 'I'm Kash Vialli. I'm the new king of these streets. And when I'm done with Santino, I'm taking your head off next.'

Kash didn't waste a single second more and took a wild swing aimed directly at Marco's head. Rex gasped, and it felt like time stood still as the sharp blade headed directly for Marco's neck.

But Marco had seen the move coming a mile away.

Marco side-stepped and then rounded up to Kash's side and hit him with a gut-busting kick to the ribs. Kash was immediately winded and the sound of his ribs cracking echoed around the room as his machete dropped out of his hand.

'Fuck. You. Asshole,' Kash said, breathless and on his knees, desperately scrabbling around to pick up his machete. 'You'll never beat me. Never...'

'Boy, look away,' Marco said. 'I'm not kidding. This ends here and now. And trust me, you don't need to see what happens next. Go and stand with Aleksei.'

Rex did as he was told and went over to Aleksei who put his arm around Rex and walked out of the room with him.

'Is my Daddy about to...' Rex said.

'He sure is,' Aleksei replied. 'This is the life we live. Kash played with fire and he's about to go up in smoke. Marco is a good man, full of honor. He'll make it quick.'

Before Rex could respond, Marco stepped out of the room.

Rex watched as Marco and Aleksei exchanged a knowing look. Rex didn't have to guess what that look meant. Kash was dead. It was all over. Or was it...

'We've taken Kash out, but this is still his place,' Marco said. 'We need to bounce right now, just in case we run into any loyal soldiers.'

'Let's go,' Aleksei said, stepping to one side and allowing Rex to fall into Marco's arms.

'Daddy, I love you,' Rex said. 'I want us to be together *forever*.'

'Me too, boy,' Marco replied. 'I want that more than anything in the world. I want to love and protect you until the end of time. But speaking of time, we don't have much of it. Let's move.'

With that, the three of them hustled their way out of the club without any trouble. It had been an intense day. But Rex was ready to move on from Kash once and for all.

And now that Marco was officially his Forever Daddy, the future had never looked brighter.

Chapter 26

Marco

A couple of days past after the showdown with Kash, and life was returning to normal. Well, as normal as life for a member of the Mafia ever could be.

But despite business resuming with his planning of the bank heist, Marco was beginning to feel settled in his love life again. Having Rex in his penthouse without the threat of Kash around to bother them any longer was a brilliant feeling.

Marco had ensured to check in with Rex often to make sure he wasn't in shock or feeling any trauma from what had happened. Rex, to his credit, had taken it all remarkably in his stride. Rex would never be a Mafia man himself, but he understood that sometimes bad things had to happen to make a situation good again.

Just like Marco, Rex had lost a parent at a young age. It was a tragedy for both of them, and yet both of them had come out of it on the other side. Now that they were together, they were able to share their experiences and grow together. Marco could see too that while him and Rex had shared bonds from their pasts, it was very much the future that they needed to look forward too – a future *together.*

With the sound of the busy city at night outside, Marco leaned back in his office chair and looked at the computer screen. Everything was coming together. Soon, Marco was confident that he would be pulling off one of the biggest bank heists in history.

Marco finished up the work and decided that it was time to shut the computer off for the evening and spend some quality time with his boy.

This can wait.

I've planned enough.

This bank won't know what's hit it...

Marco got up from his desk and walked into the living area. The sight of Rex lying on the floor in nothing but his blue and white sailing themed pajamas was a sight to behold. Rex's lean, athletic body looked all snuggly and warm as Rex lay in front of the roaring fire, playing with his stuffies.

'Room for a Daddy to join?' Marco said, a smile on his face as he walked over toward Rex.

'Yay! You're done with work!' Rex giggled, the look on his face and lightness in his voice making it clear he was in Littlespace. 'Come play!'

Marco made his way over toward Rex and got down on the thick rug and began to play along with Rex. The stuffies were apparently exploring an undiscovered planet and having a great time of it too...

'On this planet there are chocolate waterfalls and the sun is one giant popsicle,' Rex giggled, moving Ozzy across the floor with one hand and a purple elephant called Boom in the other. 'The stuffies are searching for a lost crystal and they need a Daddy to help them find it!'

'Looks like a job for me,' Marco grinned, taking a tiger and a lion stuffie in each hand and walking them along the enormous couch. 'Come on, guys, I think I've found something!'

Marco hadn't played with a boy like this before, but it felt so natural to him. Marco's fear had always been that he was too serious to play like this, that the nature of his work made him too grounded in reality. But there was something so fun and full of joy about it that Marco couldn't resist getting fully involved in it.

'Are there any baddies on this planet?' Rex said, snuggling up close to Marco. 'I'm not afraid if there are, but maybe some of the stuffies might be.'

'There used to be boy,' Marco said. 'But I blasted them all away into space. This is the happiest, safest planet in the whole galaxy.'

'What about the whole universe?' Rex replied sweetly.

'Yup, the whole universe too,' Marco chuckled.

'What's the planet called?' Rex said.

'You decide, boy,' Marco said, running his hand through Rex's soft, floppy hair.

'I want to call it... Marco-Rex 1,' Rex giggled, blushing slightly as Marco kissed him on his forehead. 'But Daddy...'

Marco had a feeling that he knew what Rex was about to say. Only moments earlier, Marco had noticed that the diaper underneath Rex's pajamas was looking awfully heavy.

'I made a pee-pee,' Rex said. 'I think I need changing.'

'No problem, astronaut,' Marco said. 'Even space explorers need their wet butt's changed from time to time. Come on, I'll carry you to the international diaper changing station.'

With that, Marco picked Rex up and flew him over toward the changing table on the other side of the large, open plan living space.

'Looks like a full one,' Marco said, pulling Rex's pajama bottoms down and opening up his thick, fluffy diaper. 'Not to worry, nothing that a quick clean, powder and fresh diaper won't solve. We'll be back exploring on Marco-Rex 1 in no time.'

Rex giggled and it brought a joy to Marco's heart that for so long had thought might evade him forever. Every moment with Rex was a joy, and now that they had removed Kash Vialli from the equation there were nothing but blue skies and happiness in their future together.

But Marco wanted to make sure of something...

'Boy, I know you said you wanted me to be your Forever Daddy,' Marco said, his voice open-hearted. 'But that was in the heat of the moment. It's okay if now the dust has settled you feel differently or just want some more time to see how things go.'

'Is that how you feel?' Rex said, an uncertain look in his eyes.

'Me? Hell no,' Marco replied. 'I've wanted to be your Forever Daddy for a *long* time. But you're the one who matters. And I won't mind if now you've been able to process the Kash thing, you want to take it slow.'

'No! I want to take it *fast*,' Rex giggled. 'I want us to shoot off into space at a million, billion miles per hour. I want us to go faster than the speed of light. I want us to be together forever, Daddy.'

Marco nodded and smiled.

Hearing Rex speak those words with such enthusiasm and from the bottom of his heart felt like nothing else Marco had ever experienced. It was better than any bank heist Marco had pulled off, and worth a lot more too.

Rex's love was priceless.

The cherry on top of the cake was the fact that Rex had helped Marco explore his kinks too. Rex was someone that Marco could trust, and the kind of boy who instinctively knew what true loyalty was. Rex was the perfect package as far as Marco was concerned, and there wasn't another boy in the whole of New York City who could compare.

Marco and Rex returned to their game of space exploration down on the floor by the fire. It may have been a cold night outside, but Marco and Rex felt as warm and cozy together as was humanly possible – and that was without even taking the roaring fire into account.

'I think this calls for one thing, and one thing only,' Marco said, a grin on his face.

'What, Daddy?' Rex said, a look of intrigue on his sweet face.

'Intergalactic hot chocolates with alien marshmallows,' Marco bellowed. 'After all, a Daddy and his boy need to stay fueled on their space mission, right?'

Rex smiled a beautiful smile and nodded before getting back to playing with his stuffies. For Marco, the ultimate dream had come true.

A Mafia Daddy and his perfect boy together, playing and having fun. It was the perfect scene and the happiest that Marco had ever felt in his whole life.

Chapter 27

Rex

A month passed and Rex was like a Little in the candy store. Life was perfect, and each day was full of fun, love, and just about everything that a Little like Rex could wish for.

Rex was loving being back at the *Peachy Playpen*, each work shift full of smiling faces, laughter, and good spirits. Rex loved nothing more than waking up in the morning and having breakfast with his Daddy Marco before the two of them set off to work.

Of course, the nature of Marco and Rex's jobs couldn't have been any more different, but that didn't matter to Rex. In many ways, it was fun that their jobs were so different as it meant that there was always plenty to talk about over dinner.

Rex knew that there were aspects to Marco's work that it was best he didn't know about. That was simply the kind of life that Marco lived, and Rex wasn't going to judge it. Plus, Rex knew that his Daddy was an honorable man who only did the *really* bad stuff when he had no other choice.

As Rex munched on his space-themed cereal that morning, he looked across to the table to see Marco quietly sipping on his espresso. Something was different about Marco though, he seemed more at peace than he had in quite a long time.

Rex thought he knew why Marco seemed like he did, but wanted to ask to make double sure...

'Daddy, what time did you get home last night?' Rex said, wiping a little drop of chocolatey milk off the corner of his mouth. 'I think I was asleep before you got home.'

Marco smiled. He looked a little bit tired, but there was a spark in his eyes too.

'You certainly were asleep before I got home,' Marco said. 'I only got back in an hour ago in fact.'

'Does that mean...'

'It does,' Marco grinned. 'We pulled it off. The biggest heist in the history of New York City. Everything went exactly to plan. Just like I hoped it would. We worked as a team, no one got hurt on either side, and we came away with the booty.'

'Booty?' Rex giggled. 'You mean like my booty?'

'No, boy,' Marco said, rolling his eyes. 'I mean like gold, cash, crypto codes, and even some diamonds too.'

'Wowzers, that's awesome,' Rex said, his mind spinning at the thought of his Daddy creeping out of a bank with big bags of gold. 'How did Aleksei do?'

'He's a great driver,' Marco said. 'And the good news is that I think we'll be working together a bit more from now on. But that's Mafia business. Top secret for Daddies!'

'*Naaaaaw*! No fair!' Rex pleaded, grumpily shoveling a big spoon of cereal into his mouth.

'Don't worry, you'll know more when it's safe to know more,' Marco smiled. 'But tell me, how is the preparation for the party later?'

Rex smiled. The party was a joint celebration for his and Marco's birthdays. Only a week – and many years – separated their birthdays and Marco decided that it might be fun to have a joint party at the *Peachy Playpen*.

Rex was of course delighted by this suggestion and had taken it upon himself to organize everything. To Rex's delight, all of their friends were able to attend and if Rex had anything to do with it, it was going to be the biggest, best, and most fun party in the whole of the city.

'I think this party is going to be…. *incredible*,' Rex said, a smile on his face that said more than a thousand words would be able to.

'Well with you running it, I don't doubt it boy,' Marco replied, finishing off his espresso. 'Now, with only an hour's sleep in the bank, I hope you don't mind but I'm going to have a nice relaxing bath and then catch up on some sleep. I'm not as young as you, I need to make sure I get my beauty sleep!'

'You mean your *Daddy* sleep,' Rex giggled.

'Same thing, right?' Marco said. 'And don't even think about sassing me. I may be exhausted, but I'm still fit and ready to warm that butt of yours.'

'Tee-hee, okay Daddy,' Rex said. 'Rest up and come and meet me at the *Peachy Playpen* all fresh and ready for the party.'

'Sounds like a plan,' Marco said, getting up from the table and leaning over Rex and planting a soft kiss on his cheek. 'I love you boy. You make me so happy.'

'Same, Daddy,' Rex said, his cheeks glowing with pride and love for just about the most perfect Daddy he could ever have wished for.

As Marco walked toward the bathroom, Rex finished off his cereal and hopped up to drink a big glass of water and take his vitamins. There was a busy morning of prep ahead of Rex if he was going to make this party pop!

* * *

The *Peachy Playpen* was full of life. Rex had excelled and absolutely everyone in attendance was having a wonderful time.

The theme to the party was Silk & Sports, a subtle nod to both Rex and Marco's preferred kinks. This meant that some Daddies were dressed in their favorite sportswear, and some of them in silky pajamas. The same was true of the Littles. Everyone was comfortable in what they were wearing and it all contributed to a fun atmosphere.

Rex was wearing the MMA shorts that Marco had brought for him, while Marco was wearing a super-silky pajama set – the only difference being that underneath his pajama bottoms he also had a pair of soft, frilly and extremely sensual panties on.

The panties may have been Marco and Rex's little secret, but the truth was that no one at the party would have judged them for it.

With the music pumping and the Littles having fun, Rex walked over toward Marco to see what was going on with him and his Daddy friends...

'Are you all talking about business?' Rex said, arching his eyebrow. 'At your birthday party? That's *too* Daddy.'

'Ha, well, guilty as charged,' Marco laughed, exchanging a knowing look with Dante and Rocco. 'We were just saying that we've recruited three new men to travel over from the West coast. They're good Mafia men in need of a new family to join.'

'Yup, and they're Daddies too,' Rocco said, looking very macho in his football shirt and tight, white shorts.

'Each one with a different skill set,' Dante added. 'And each one in need of a boy too. So, if you know of any one of your Little friends who might want to become a Mafia man's boy...'

'*Hmmm*, I think I might!' Rex said, looking over toward the three Littles he made friends with on that fateful day he came to the Peachy Playpen.

'Love isn't as simple as that,' Marco said. 'the new Mafia Daddies will have to find their own way in love. We got lucky. And we had to battle through some tough moments together. But we did it.'

'We sure did, Daddy!' Rex giggled. 'And it looks like Aleksei might be about to, as well!'

The Mafia Daddies and Rex look toward Aleksei who was wearing silky pajama shorts and nothing else. Aleksei was playing a game of tag with two Littles, both of whom looked like they were *very* happy to be playing with the Russian mobster.

'He turned out to be a good guy,' Marco said. 'And one hell of a driver.'

'Sure did,' Rocco laughed. 'And now we've got another ally. It's not going to be easy building a power base that will allow us to move away from the elders and stand independent.'

'But if anyone can, it's us,' Dante said, holding his beer aloft. 'Here's to the Mafia Daddies. It's us three, and soon our new friends, against the world!'

'And your Littles too!' Rex added, holding his juice box in the air to toast as well.

The Mafia Daddies and their boys had found love and hope for their own independent future too. But that was business. All that Rex and Marco could think about in that moment was being together.

'So, how about we sneak off for a bit to one of the private fun rooms?' Marco said, a noticeable bulge forming at the front of his pajamas.

'Daddy!' Rex giggled. 'Yes, a million times yes!'

The two of them held hands and took one quick look at everyone having fun. Laughter, smiling faces, and Littles and Daddies were having the best time in each and every direction.

This was their party to celebrate not only Rex and Marco's birthdays, but their love for one another too. And now it was time to celebrate in the most private, fun, and kinkiest way possible.

'I love you Daddy,' Rex said, looking up at Marco's gruff, loving, and utterly handsome face.

'And I love you too, boy,' Marco replied, gently squeezing Rex's hand. 'I love you too.'

MORE MAFIA DADDIES NYC

I hope you enjoyed Avenge Me Daddy, the third book in my new Mafia Daddies NYC series.

Check out all six Mafia Daddy books below, have you read them all yet? Please show your support and order / preorder them today!

TRAIN ME DADDY

CONTROL ME DADDY

AVENGE ME DADDY

HUNT ME DADDY

TEACH ME DADDY

FINISH ME DADDY

I'm so excited about this series, there will be even more books on their way - but while you wait, keep reading and check out the rest of my catalogue...

MORE ZACK

Thank you *so much* for reading, I hope you had a great time!

If you'd love a **steamy & cute FREE STORY**, please sign up to my newsletter either by clicking **HERE** or copying and pasting the link below into your browser:

https://bit.ly/3KME5ra

I promise to never send spam emails. Only notifications of my upcoming releases and some super-fun little extras too!

Read the first **GRUFF GUARDIAN DADDIES** books:

DADDY RESCUE AT LITTLE RAPIDS

DADDY DANGER AT LITTLE RAPIDS

Have you checked out my first **Uptown Heat** book yet?

CHANGING HAYDEN

Read my famous **HERO DADDIES** series here:

SAVING DYLAN

GUARDING CASPER

CLAIMING MILO

TAMING TIMOTHEE

OWNING AIDAN

DEFENDING JUSTIN

HOLIDAY HERO DADDY

Or why not try my co-authored **LITTLES OF CAPE DADDY** novellas?

CHECK OUT ALL 6 BOOKS HERE

And not forgetting my much-loved **Little Club NYC** series...

READ ALL 5 BOOKS HERE

I hugely appreciate all **ratings and reviews on Amazon** as they help my books get seen! Every single rating and review is hugely appreciated by me – thank you!

Following me on **Facebook** & **BookBub** yet? If not, come and join me! Get involved for news, updates and DDlb fun!

I love to hear from readers too, so please feel free to email me at zackwishauthor@gmail.com

Thank you and have a great day wherever you are!

Zack XoXo

Printed in Great Britain
by Amazon

25115075R00129